JACQUES VON KAT

On the Other Side of Alive

First published by Broadthumb Publishing 2020

Copyright © 2020 by Jacques Von Kat

All rights reserved. No part of this publication may be reproduced, stored or transmitted in any form or by any means, electronic, mechanical, photocopying, recording, scanning, or otherwise without written permission from the publisher. It is illegal to copy this book, post it to a website, or distribute it by any other means without permission.

This novel is entirely a work of fiction. The names, characters and incidents portrayed in it are the work of the author's imagination. Any resemblance to actual persons, living or dead, events or localities is entirely coincidental.

Jacques Von Kat asserts the moral right to be identified as the author of this work.

First edition

This book was professionally typeset on Reedsy.
Find out more at reedsy.com

In loving memory of Mick (JJ)

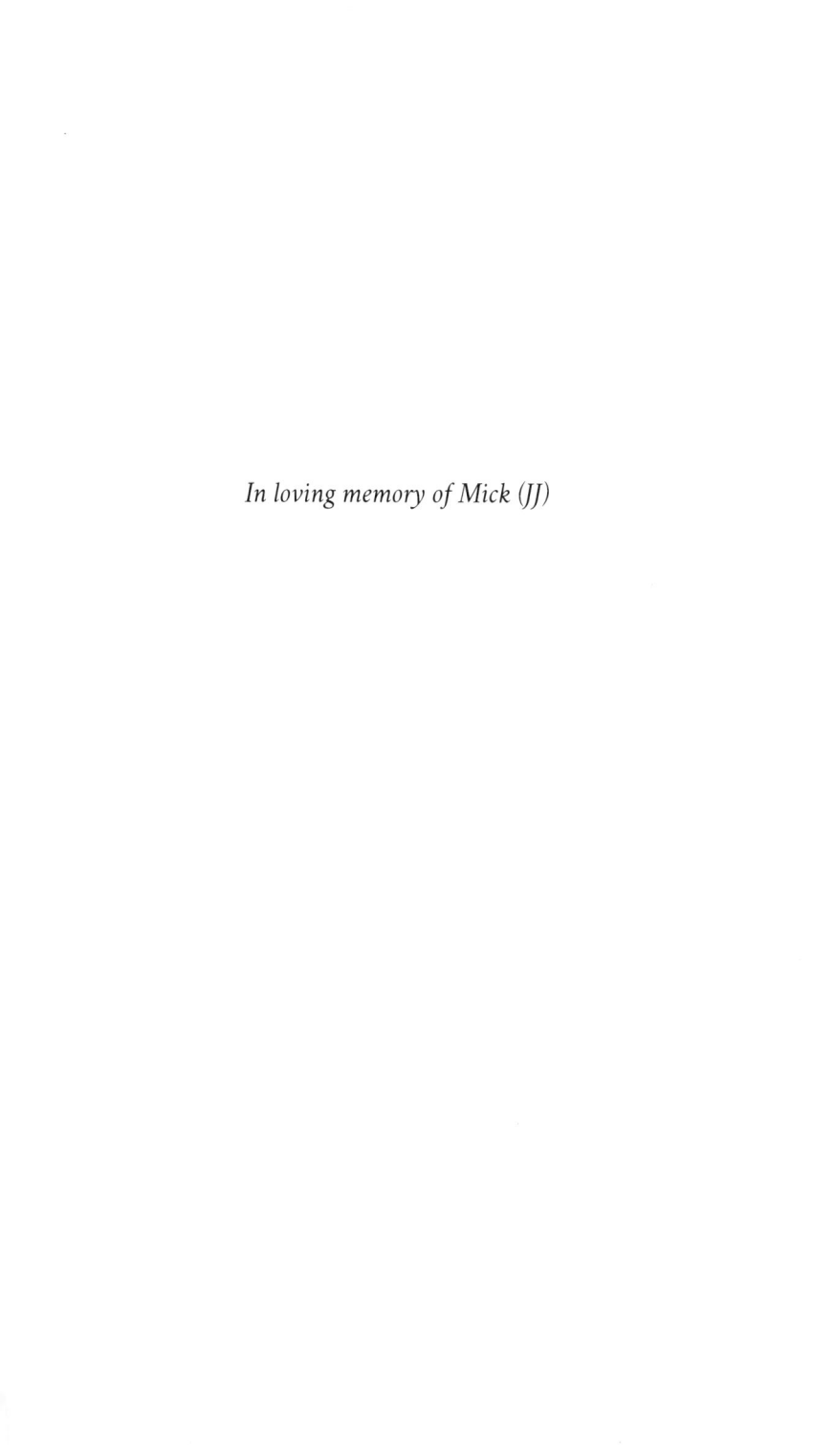

Acknowledgement

First of all, we have to say thank you to our editor, Liz. You really helped us get the book to where we wanted it to be.

Also thank you to Shell and Alyssa for helping to name one of the characters. A special thank you to Bethan, Sue and Tracey.

Lastly, thank you to all our family and friends who have supported us on this journey. It really means the world to us.

Chapter One

Looking back, I wonder if I would have learnt all I know now if I had said no to coming back. Would I still hate Mondays or grow to love them wherever I had ended up?

You might wonder why I hated that specific day. Well, I had lots of reasons to detest it, but one overshadowed them all. One fateful Monday would set the course for the rest of my existence.

* * *

One ordinary April Monday, rain descended upon my little world. I'd got soaked cycling into work, forcing me to spend five minutes drying off my tights under the hand dryer in the staff toilets. This made me late for the weekly plan that I reluctantly presented every Monday morning.

The plan never changed from week to week, month to month, but my manager insisted on it, despite the persistent groans and contagious yawns of my colleagues.

I smoothed down my hair as best I could and made my way to the conference room.

'Nice of you to join us, Caroline,' the office bitch commented—though some might call her Sophia. She tapped her pen on her notepad obnoxiously as I made my way to the lectern with my head bent low so my hair fell over the flush spreading across my cheeks.

I fiddled with the wires connected to the projector as Lyndsey brought in my notes and placed them by my paper cup of water.

Sophia jostled her chair, forcing it to bang against the conference-room table. My cup wobbled, splashing water over my notes. This wasn't the first time Sophia had done this; I had now taken to drinking water instead of coffee in the meeting, and it was the sole reason why Lyndsey printed out two sets of notes.

I whispered a quiet 'Thank you' as I loaded the presentation, retrieved the second set of notes, and cleared my throat. When I looked up, I caught Lyndsey's eye where she stood by the door, and she gave me a warm smile. She knew how much I hated standing in front of everyone.

'Right, here we go,' I said confidently and proceeded with the presentation.

* * *

'If there aren't any questions, I'll see you all next week,' I concluded thirty minutes later.

Everyone rose in unison and shuffled out except for Lyndsey and me. As I packed up, she loitered on the other side of the lectern. When the door softly clicked shut behind the last of my colleagues, she said, 'You really should say something to her,' with a hand on her hip.

'Who? Sophia?' I shrugged. 'What's the point? She'll never

change.'

'You could at least tell Clare,' she said, her green eyes wide with innocence.

Lyndsey had a lot to learn about life in this office. She had only been with us a few months, but we had formed an instant friendship.

What Lyndsey didn't know about Sophia was her sheer nastiness. Not long before Lyndsey joined us, Sophia had tried to start an affair with the printing manager. He refused to entertain her advances, but she wouldn't take no for an answer and turned vicious with her pursuit. In the end, he had to report her for sexual harassment. Clare didn't take it any further than giving Sophia a severe reprimand.

I don't know what was wrong with Sophia, but this wasn't the first time she had made life hard for a team member. I had to wonder why Clare didn't finish her. Did she have something on her?

I huffed. 'Nah. That's the last thing I want to be: the office tattletale.'

'I guess…' Lyndsey sighed, turning for the door. 'So, what did you do this weekend?'

'Nothing much. James was busy with work,' I said, piling my things into my arms to follow her out.

'Again?'

'Yeah, but it's my parents thirtieth wedding anniversary this weekend, and he's promised he'll have no distractions.'

She nodded. 'That's great,' she said with little enthusiasm. I raised an eyebrow at her as we reached my desk, but she continued on to her own a few desks over.

'Talk later,' she mouthed to me.

And so I sank onto my chair. While I waited for my desktop

to boot up, I looked around with the same modest amazement I felt every morning; I had the best job in the best office in town, and not even a petty bully like Sophia could take that away from me.

No expense had been spared in the fittings. The office was open plan with orthopaedic adjustable seats and desks, and lockers and showers with fancy changing rooms. My manager, Clare, had made sure the lighting was perfect to protect her staff's eyes, and the office shut once a month for the carpets to be cleaned. There was even a creche for those with children.

I completed my morning to-do list, then headed out for an early lunch, since it had stopped raining. I collected James's suits on a Monday, which I hated just as much as I hated giving the weekly plan.

I arrived at the dry cleaners just as the heavens opened.

'Not again…' I muttered.

I stood in the queue and snuck a bite of my chicken sandwich as I waited, praying the store manager wasn't hanging around.

I peeped over the shoulder of the man in front of me.

Big mistake.

'Mrs Rushton, you are right on time.' The manager smiled, flashing all his teeth. 'Come on down, these other customers won't mind.'

I'm sure they do mind…, I thought.

'Sorry,' I mumbled as I walked past the others, my face flushed like a beacon at their mutters and grumbles.

'You look lovely this morning, Mrs Rushton. Have you done yourself up specially to see me?'

I grimaced. 'How much do I owe you?'

'A touch of red wouldn't go amiss,' he answered.

I shuddered as a woman tutted loudly behind me. *Why do I*

CHAPTER ONE

put myself through this every week?

I paid and hurried out of there into the rain to get my second soaking of the day.

I didn't bother drying again when I returned to the office, convincing myself I'd be in for another downpour when I left work. Just as I settled back into my seat, Clare called me over to her desk.

Wondering what she might want, I patted down my hair and straightened my clothes as I made my way over. God knows what I looked like. As I passed Lyndsey's desk, I caught her eye and nodded towards the toilets.

'Caroline, darling, take a seat.'

Clare pulled her swivel chair to the side to sit closer to me. She wore the outfit I envied from afar and wished I could pull off: a silk blouse in her favourite colour, teal; a leather pencil skirt to show off her hourglass figure; and killer heels. Her blonde hair hung in perfect curls around her petite head, and her olive eyes quickly scanned my appearance.

She tilted her head. 'Sweetheart, what happened to you?'

'Oh.' I laughed nervously. 'I had to cycle in today. I got a drenching this morning and at lunch.'

'I've got a change of clothes in my locker if you want?' she said, reaching for her key.

'No, it's fine. I'll soon dry off.' *And there's no way I could pull off your outfits.*

Clare preferred to accentuate her figure, whereas I favoured comfort over style. I wasn't body confident like she was.

'Well, if you're sure...' She dropped her keys. 'We still on for lunch on Wednesday?'

'Yes, of course.' I fidgeted in my seat, crossing my legs, hyper aware of how her eyes kept flicking down to my sopping ballet flats. 'So… what can I do for you, Clare?'

'Relax. I know I don't call you over often, but there's nothing to worry about. You're my best worker.'

I relaxed a little. I didn't like being away from my desk for too long; I liked to mind my own business and get on with my work. That had always been my motto. Well, my dad's, really: keep your head down, finish every task by close of play, and you will go far.

'How's that hubby of yours? Still working a lot?'

'Yeah, he's good. Still busy.' *Get on with it; I've got work to do.*

'Great.' She smiled, showing off her bright, white veneers. 'Well, my reason for calling you over is the Chailox group are wanting someone to head up their market research figures for the next financial year. A bit late, I know, but I want you to run it. *And…* if you do a good job with this, then you'll be in line to make partner.'

'What?' I leant forwards, suddenly much more awake than I had been. 'Are you serious? That'll make me the youngest partner in the company's history.'

'*Dead serious*, Caroline.' Clare smiled, though I noted a strange tone to her voice. 'Now, it *will* mean some late nights and nights away. Will James be okay with that?'

'He'll be fine. He gets called away often, so I'm sure we can make it work.'

If he can do it, then so can I!

She raised a perfectly drawn eyebrow. 'Well, that's great. Are sure you don't want to discuss it with him first? You can always get him down here,' she said, twiddling her necklace. It looked new.

'No, not at all. I'm eager to get started straight away. Can I pick my own team?' I asked.

CHAPTER ONE

Dad was right; keeping your head down does pay off, and it's so much better than being a kiss ass.

'Sure. You best select your team right away and get started. You're behind already. I'll send the files over to you now,' Clare said, then she shimmied her chair back around her desk and clicked her mouse a few times.

'Not a problem. I'll get on it now. And thank you, Clare, you don't know what this means to me.'

She nodded and smiled, and I stood up feeling light as a feather. Instead of heading back to my desk, I went to the toilets where Lyndsey was waiting for me. We had an unspoken rule where we would meet there when there was gossip to discuss.

'What was all that about?' she asked.

'Well...' I exhaled past the grin threatening my lips, 'Clare wants me to head up a new contract, and if it all goes well, I'm going to make partner!'

'Oh my god!' She took my hands, and we did a little jig. 'That's amazing, you totally deserve it.'

'Thank you. I can't believe it,' I said, leaning back against the sinks. 'Guess a celebration is in order. Maybe this horrid day is finally turning around for me.'

'What do you mean *horrid*?'

'I've got drenched twice today. Sophia embarrassed me this morning, and the manager at the dry cleaners gets creepier every week...' I shuddered again.

'I don't know why you continue to use that place,' she said, reapplying her pink lip gloss.

'Because they're quick and cheap.' I shrugged.

She paused in applying her make-up to look across at me. 'You're both working; can't you afford somewhere else?'

'You'd think, but I don't know where all our money's been going, lately.'

Lyndsey shrugged as if to say, 'I'm all out of suggestions.'

'I guess I should ring James,' I said, heading back to the door. 'See you back in there.'

When I re-entered the office, girlish laughter made me glance over at Clare. She was laughing like a giddy schoolgirl as she twirled her hair between her fingers. Her other hand pressed her phone to her ear. I chuckled quietly as I settled at my desk and picked up my work phone.

I had both James's direct line and mobile number on speed dial. I tried his direct line first (no answer), then his mobile, which was engaged.

Lyndsey exited the toilet as I put my phone down. She raised an eyebrow in Clare's direction, who was still giggling quietly into her phone, oblivious to the rest of the office.

An instant message popped up on my computer screen.

'Who's Clare talking to?' Lyndsey asked.

'God knows,' I typed back. *'She's had a lot of personal calls these past few weeks, though.'*

'A new man???'

'Dunno. I'll quiz her on Wednesday.'

I tried James again; still engaged.

The third number on my speed dial was my best friend, Tamara. I dialled her number, and she picked up on the third ring. I was the second number on her list.

'Hey, girl. How's it going?' she answered.

'Hey! I'm good. How're you and Eliza?'

'We're good. Having a nightmare with childcare this week. You've got all this to come. What's happening on that front, by the way?'

CHAPTER ONE

'Nothing yet, but it's only been a couple of months,' I said as I quickly typed an email inviting Tyler and Marie to join my team on the Chailox group contract.

'Anyway, to what do I owe the pleasure on this dreary Monday?' she asked.

'I'm up for promotion,' I whispered, then pulled my hand away from my ear as Tamara squealed down the line.

'I knew you'd get there!' I caught her saying as I repositioned the receiver.

'Yeah... it's great.'

'You don't sound very happy,' she said, her voice thick with concern.

'Oh, I am.' I sighed. 'I just wanted to let James know, but I can't get hold of him.'

'I'm sure he's busy with work. Don't worry, you'll tell him later.'

'You're right.' I glanced at my mobile as it vibrated across my desk. 'In fact, I think he just messaged me.'

'Great. Talk to you soon.'

'Tell Eliza I love her.'

'Will do. Laters!'

As I hung up, I picked up my phone with my other hand. Sure enough, it was James:

'Sorry, I was on a call. Will phone you back in 5. Xoxo.'

I sucked on my cheek and drummed my fingers on my desk as I half-heartedly looked through the files Clare had sent. When my phone rang, I picked it up on the first ring.

'Hi, Caroline, sorry I missed you.'

'Not to worry,' I muttered.

'I'll pick you up at three to save you getting drenched. Right, got to go!'

The call ended before I had chance to tell him my news.

* * *

Three o'clock arrived, and he pulled up right on time. He told me to get in while he folded my bike and placed it in the boot, then hung his suits in the back of the car.

James Brown played on the radio.

'Look on the back seat,' James said as he jumped back in the car and started to drive.

I looked behind me; a bottle of red wine lolled from side to side with the car's motion, and a dozen pink and cream roses dripped tiny droplets on the upholstery.

'Aw, you shouldn't have!' I beamed at him. 'It's not a special occasion, is it?'

'You tell me,' he said with a wink, then he shook his head like a wet dog, deliberately sending drops of water everywhere. I laughed as I wiped the rain off my face.

'You know I can't drink too much while we're trying,' I said.

'A little glass won't hurt.'

I smirked. 'Okay, just a little one…'

James paused for a moment. 'This song's right, you know.'

I tilted my head to look at him. 'Right about what?'

'My world would be nothing without my woman in it.'

I smiled at him, my earlier annoyance having fluttered away. I couldn't contain it any longer, and I almost burst as I filled him in on my soon-to-be-partner status.

'That's great, Caroline!' he said as he reached for my hand and planted a soft, wet kiss on my fingers.

My husband had been more attentive than usual these past few months. Buying me small gifts and flowers, running bubble baths surrounded by candles, cooking dinner… I'd mentioned the change in James to my friends on a rare night out together.

'Are you complaining?' one had asked.

'It's more than we get!' another added.

As James sang along with the radio, I sat back and considered how lucky I'd been to find a man like him, and I found myself staring at him.

His blond hair had darkened with the rain, and his usual spikes drooped down. A single raindrop rolled over his face onto his soft lips and landed on his muscular thigh, and I pictured what he had in store for me that evening—if he didn't get another call from the office, that was.

A text coming through the speaker brought me back from my daydream.

'*Text from CJ: We still on for Friday Night?*' said the female robotic voice.

I scowled. 'Who's CJ, and what's happening Friday?'

'You remember CJ, don't you?' he said quickly.

I didn't answer. I couldn't recall any of James's friends being called CJ.

'Carl Juggins. He was at our wedding?' James continued.

'Sorry, I don't remember him.'

'Well, we're having a couple of drinks Friday night. A little catchup, that's all.'

'First I've heard about it.' I folded my arms.

'I thought I'd told you,' he said, then he switched the radio off.

'Have you remembered we're going to my parents first thing Saturday?'

'Sure, don't worry,' he reached for my hand, but I snatched

it away.

We continued the journey in silence.

* * *

James disappeared into his office as soon as we arrived home and didn't emerge for another hour. When he finally did, I was sat in the living room, losing myself in the final hours of daytime TV and scrolling through the news feed on social media.

'Why don't you have a quick shower, and I'll take you out for steak to celebrate,' he said and kissed the top of my head.

I twisted my neck to look up at him. 'Really? What if work rings?'

'I'll turn my phone off.'

I hopped up from the sofa and pecked him on the cheek. 'I'd love that.'

He caught my waist as I pulled away. 'Wear your *Meat is Murder* t-shirt. I love the looks on their faces when you stroll in wearing that.'

I laughed. 'You got it, babe.' I made a move to leave, then stopped at the bottom of the stairs. 'Oh, what about your car? The garage said to pick it up this evening.'

'I'll tell them we're busy,' he said. 'We'll pick it up tomorrow.'

Thirty minutes later, we left in my car and made it to the town centre. I watched through the window as yet another downpour graced the town. But unlike this morning, I wasn't so irritated. I turned my head to see James smiling at me fondly, one hand on the steering wheel, the other patting a rhythm on his thigh. The traffic lights turned red just as another text came through the speakers from CJ.

CHAPTER ONE

James's expression changed.

Screeching tyres covered the robotic voice, and everything started to spin. With the crunch of metal, my whole life whizzed before me in reverse, and in the corner of my eye, my deceased grandmother reached out for me.

As fast as the crash happened, everything stilled.

Invisible hands pulled and yanked at my body, trying to free me from the wreckage. With a final pull that turned my stomach and made my eyes bulge, I landed on a clean white floor with a thud.

Chapter Two

'Shit!' I scrambled to my feet and patted myself down to check for wounds but found none. Then I looked around.

I'd been taken to a large, clean, white room and left on my own.

My mind whirled; it didn't smell like a hospital, nor sound like one; it was too quiet. And when I checked, there wasn't any equipment. Not even a bandage or a bed.

It made no sense. I could have sworn people had pulled me from the car. I wondered if I'd passed out in the ambulance on the way here or had a manic episode and the hospital staff had put me in this room to protect myself.

I realised I still had my handbag over my shoulder, so I rummaged around for my phone to call James. I fumbled with the touchscreen and somehow managed to call him, but the line never connected.

'James, James!' I yelled in frustration. His name echoed around the room with no reply.

I tried to walk to the edge of the room, but as I did, the walls moved farther away from me.

'What's going on?' I shouted, but only my echo replied.

I sat on the floor and felt around for any hidden trapdoors;

CHAPTER TWO

there had to be a way out of this place.

But there was nothing. Not even a fleck of paint to peel back.

I got up and paced the white floor, then I clenched my fists and yelled out again. My shouts turned into screams, and my screams into sobs. Eventually, I crumpled to the ground.

Someone yelled from behind me: 'We've got another one!'

Another what? I thought. I looked towards the voice, and a man was heading towards me dressed in a Hawaiian shirt, shorts, and crocs.

For some reason, the stranger chuckled to himself, as though my presence there was amusing, but all I could think was *Why is this man wearing crocs?*

I reasoned with myself and concluded I was dreaming, still lying amongst the wreckage of our vehicle. Whatever the situation, I had to wake up and get back to James.

The man hovered over me and shouted again: 'Raff, are you listening? We have another one.'

I checked the room again but couldn't see anyone.

'Another what?' I asked. 'And who are you talking to?'

'Let me introduce myself; I'm Azrael,' he said, then bowed. 'But you may call me Az.'

I got to my feet. I'd spent more time on the floor here than I had upright. 'Oh-kay. But *who* are you? Where am I? Where's James? What—'

Az raised his palms. 'Woah, slow down, Caroline.'

Before I could ask how he knew my name, another man appeared from nowhere wearing a similar outfit to Az.

'Oh goodie, another one.' Raff's tone was laced with sarcasm. 'We were just about to limbo,' he whined.

My pulse pounded, and my head thudded. 'Another what?' I

shouted. 'Will one of you please tell me what's going on!'

'Just relax,' Az soothed. 'There is no easy way to say this, but you've died.'

'Hah,' I laughed dryly. 'Yeah, right. Now, if you could show me the way out of this funny farm, I'll be off. I need to find my husband.'

The duo exchanged bemused glances.

'You really are dead,' said Raff.

'No, I'm not.'

'Yes, you are.'

'No, I'm not!' I insisted.

'You are,' Az and Raff chimed together.

'But… I can't be. I can still feel my body working, my heart is beating, I—' I had to be alive. I was loved and needed. And above all, I had consciousness, *didn't I?*

'Those are just remnants, sweetie. Your mind will struggle with the transition, but it will soon fade away,' said Az.

I sank to the floor once more and stared up at these strangers as I tried to digest the bombshell they had handed to me.

My mind worked overtime as hundreds of questions swirled in my brain. Could I believe these two strangers? Had I really been ripped from my life so prematurely and cruelly a mere twenty-five years in?

I thought about all the things I hadn't done yet, wondered how James would cope without me, how would my parents handle the news, what Chailox would do without me at the helm. *No*, I shook my head, *not that part…*

I blinked fast, hoping the action would wake me from this nightmare.

Raff jigged about on the spot. 'Hurry her up, will you? I want to get back to the party.'

CHAPTER TWO

'Alright, just give her a few minutes,' Az hissed.

My momentary breakdown waned, and as I started to compose myself, I began to hiccup. *How can I have hiccups if I'm dead?* I questioned. I needed more proof.

Still sat, I held out my arm. 'Will you pinch me?' I asked Az.

'Why?'

'I want to be sure I'm not dreaming.'

Raff stormed over and pinched me firmly on my right arm.

'Ouch!' I yelled.

'Satisfied?' asked Az.

'Well, I guess so since I'm still here.' I stared at the men in front of me. 'This can't be happening…' I muttered.

'It is happening. Now, listen to me carefully; you've got a decision to make, and we don't have much time. We've got others coming in—we get overcrowded up here too,' Az said quickly and held his hand out to help me to my feet. His skin was cold and soft, and when I looked at his hand again, I noticed he had six digits instead of five.

'What decision?' I asked, trying to ignore his strange hands.

'Look, it's simple: do you want to go back to Earth or move on up there?' Raff interjected and pointed to the ceiling.

'I don't understand. I… can… go back home?' I sputtered. 'I can live again?'

'No, you won't be alive, but you can roam the Earth for a set period,' said Az. 'If you choose to move on up, you'll only get to visit now and then.'

'Roam the Earth?' I clutched my throat. 'So you mean I'll be a ghost if I—'

'WE DO NOT USE THAT WORD!' Raff thundered.

I gawped at Raff in horror at his little outburst. *If not a ghost, then what?* But I was too afraid to ask what form I would take;

I could only wonder at the problem Raff seemed to have with me.

If these two strangers were angels guarding Heaven's gates, then Raff needed to retake his customer service lessons.

Have I died or have I gone insane? I speculated.

'Yes, you are dead, and you haven't gone mad,' Az smiled.

My previously crossed arms dropped to my side, and my mouth slackened.

'Raff's problem is that he is missing the Hawaiian party, and he has been the limbo champion for the last three decades,' he continued.

'Oh, so that explains the outfits,' I muttered with a glance at Raff, who rolled his eyes.

Az nodded, then took me by the shoulders, turned me around, and we walked towards an oversized roulette table. The wheel hadn't been there earlier, but I went with it. As we got closer, I spotted three different coloured balls, almost as big as bowling balls, sat on separate stands.

'You can read my mind?' I enquired.

'Yes, when we feel it's necessary. So, as Raff told you, you have a decision to make: go back to Earth or move on up. If you decide to return to Earth, it'll only be for a set time, determined by whatever number your ball lands on.'

Of course, I wanted to go back; I was twenty-five years old, still in my prime. I wasn't ready to leave everything I knew and loved behind to move on to who knows where.

Curtis Mayfield started to sing in my head. The song was about going towards your destination. I was sure going upwards wasn't my destination, at least for now. Before nagging doubts clouded my judgement, I made a decision.

'I want to go back,' I whispered.

CHAPTER TWO

'Speak up so we can all hear!' yelled Raff.

I clenched my fists and bellowed, 'I want to go back!'

'Good, that's settled, then,' said Az. 'All decisions made are final, contrary to section four hundred and twenty-three, part five.'

'Time to spin the wheel of time, time, time!' Raff's voice echoed.

Now Az rolled his eyes.

'Okay, here we go,' he said. 'First, choose the direction you will throw the ball: left or right.'

I cocked my head. 'Does it matter?'

'Yes, of course, it matters, or we wouldn't ask,' Raff piped in.

'Fine…' I looked down at the balls. 'I choose right.'

'Good. Next, choose a colour. Yellow, orange, or green. Pick wisely, Caroline,' Az said.

'Green. I hope you aren't playing games with me.' I eyed the duo. 'I don't want to be tricked.'

'It might seem like a game, but the decisions you make now seal the fate of your destiny on the spiritual plane,' said Raff.

I had no idea what he was talking about. What was a spiritual plane?

And why would I need a destiny? I was going back to my family; they needed me. Though I still clung to the hope that this was all a hallucination, so I played along with confidence that this nightmare would eventually end.

'So, what do I do now?' I asked.

'Pick up the green ball and look underneath, that will tell you if you have selected weeks, months or years,' Az advised.

I inspected the ball, which weighed less then it looked.

'Years,' I revealed.

Az nodded. 'And you picked *right*; throw the ball anti-

19

clockwise, and we'll see where it lands.'

I threw the ball as hard as I could and watched in horror as it appeared to settle on number one, but it rattled in the groove for a moment, then bounced into number ten.

Az clapped his hands excitedly. 'Wow, good for you, honey! You've bagged yourself a fair chunk of time.'

'Thank you,' I mumbled, although I had no idea what I was thankful for. I certainly wasn't grateful for my early death.

And what of the choices I'd made? Had I made the right ones? Where would they lead me? Az seemed so happy for me, but I couldn't share in his enthusiasm.

I shuffled where I stood and looked at my feet. 'What happens now?'

'You'll go back in a moment; preparations for your return are in motion. Michael will be along soon, and he'll take you back.'

Raff bent over and touched his toes, then did a star jump. 'Can we go now? I need to prepare myself for the event.'

Az tutted and shook his head, then he turned to me. 'Is there anything you want to ask?'

Of course, I had questions for him, but I didn't want to appear stupid by asking the wrong thing. So, I asked the question that burned in my mind the most:

'What will it be like?' I asked. 'Going back, I mean…' I added quickly.

'Basically, everything will be the same as you remember,' Raff rudely interrupted as Az opened his mouth. 'Except you can only speak to others like you. Have you seen the film *Ghost*?' he asked. I nodded that I had. 'Well, it's like that,' he chuckled.

'It's not like that at all, and you know it,' said Az, hands on his hips. 'But he is right on one point; you can usually only speak

CHAPTER TWO

to others like you. Unless you come across a living person who has a gift—then they may be able to hear you and, in some cases, see you. You'll figure it out, honey, I have a good feeling about you.' He ended on a wink, then they both disappeared in a flash of pink smoke.

I stood alone, bewildered. I glanced back to where the wheel stood, but it had also vanished. I had nothing except a whole load of whiteness to stare at.

Everything had happened at record speed; I had died (although the angels hadn't totally convinced me), and I could go back in some form or another. I hadn't had the time to think about what this would mean for me when I returned, of course. The main thing was that I would be able to watch over my loved ones. What else could I do when no one can see me?

A soft voice interrupted my thoughts: 'Knock, knock...'

I did a double take at the man before me, dressed in robes of white and gold; a big step up from the outfits Az and Raff had on.

'Sorry, I took so long. Thought I should dress appropriately for the occasion,' he said, then twirled. 'I'm Michael.'

I nodded. I couldn't speak. The sight of Michael had removed my ability to form words. He was beautiful, and a brilliant blue aura surrounded him; it radiated warmth and happiness.

'Don't worry if you can't speak, I know this is all very overwhelming for you. I've got a lot to say, anyway. Caroline, I need to make sure you understand what has happened to you and what will be happening next,' said Michael as he stepped closer and lightly touched my arm.

My mind churned, but the touch of his hand slowed it down. I breathed him in; his scent reminded me of babies and chocolate-chip cookies.

'Caroline, do you understand that you have died?'

I nodded that I did, though I didn't believe it yet.

'I'm going to take you back shortly to the place you loved the most. You will get to remain on Earth for ten years and then I will come and collect you,' he said, taking me by the arm. Michael carried on with his speech as we walked through the vast whiteness. As we moved, the room closed in and the walls and ceilings sprung to life with all the colours of the rainbow.

'You must remember,' he continued, 'that you will not be able to communicate with the living unless they have a gift. If you decide to go into a person's home, be careful.' He wagged his finger. 'Don't move objects around too much or open doors when the occupants are present, as they will notice. I must warn you; if too much activity occurs in a house, the resident may seek a cleansing to rid the house of any spirits. If this occurs, you will not be able to enter again.' He stopped to face me. 'Are you still with me, Caroline?'

'Yes.' My voice quivered.

I had watched enough supernatural programmes to understand what Michael meant, but what he talked about sounded like haunting a house; I had no intention of doing that whatsoever. I wanted to return to check on my husband and family.

'Once we arrive, you will have the opportunity to change your clothes, and I highly suggest you do.' He looked me up and down with distaste. 'You will not get the chance again; you will stay in this outfit for eternity.'

I looked at the outfit I'd chosen for dinner with James. I didn't see a problem with the clothes I had on. I wore my favourite *Meat is Murder* t-shirt, a knee-length denim skirt, black tights, and converse. Clare and James had no issues with my style of clothes, so it seemed funny it would bother Michael—especially after seeing Raff and Az in crocs.

Come on; angels in *crocs*. Have you ever heard of something so ridiculous?

'Any questions, Caroline?'

I shook my head, though regretted it immediately as he took my hand and told me to close my eyes. I had a billion questions to ask, but we started to move, and though I'd closed my eyes, I detected the motion of flight as we tumbled back to Earth. The sensation was what I imagined parachute jumpers experienced as they soared through the sky, and I had to keep myself from squealing.

With a whoosh, we landed on terra-firma. I opened my eyes and found we were stood outside my old comprehensive school. There she stood in all her glory: Our Lady of the Good Shepherd Catholic School. It looked the same as the day I'd left.

I wasn't even Catholic; it was my mother who had insisted we put this school as my first choice when it came time to select a secondary school.

Until my death, I'd gone back and forth between agnosticism and atheism, though I never told my teachers my beliefs or non-beliefs.

'*What the fuck* are we doing here?' I demanded to know.

'This is your old school. You were at your happiest during your years here,' Michael said calmly, not in the least offended by my language.

I dropped my head and closed my eyes, and if Michael sensed the disappointment in me, he didn't let on.

By no means did I expect I'd be spending my ten years at

my old school—or going back to my childhood at all, for that matter.

What would my twenty-five-year-old self do with a bunch of teenage girls? Spend my days roaming my old corridors, scaring the nuns and year sevens?

'No, this isn't right. You tricked me. I might have been happy here when I was younger, but…' I sighed. 'If I had died of old age, then yes, I might have accepted being brought back here. But my family and friends are still alive. I need to be with them, to watch over them. I certainly don't want to be back here.'

'We haven't tricked you. Far from it. Coming back here is what you have chosen. Didn't Az explain what the choices meant? Here is your chance to reminisce,' he said.

'Reminisce? I'm twenty-five, not eighty-five. And no, Az didn't explain it,' I snapped.

I walked over to the school gates and peered through. Girls were sat in little groups, chatting away. Then I spotted my fifteen-year-old self; I had long, frizzy hair and NHS glasses. My friends and I were crowded around a copy of a teen-girl magazine. Now, I styled my hair in a sleek bob, wore contact lenses, and read *The New Yorker*.

I spotted Sister Mary-Jayne yelling at the popular girls; no doubt they had too much make-up on, or the length of their skirts contravened school policy. This era wasn't the place for me; I needed to be in my own time, with family.

I turned to the angel who was now stood beside me, admiring the brass knockers on the old wooden gates. 'Michael, I shouldn't be here. I don't want to live in the past. I need to be in my own time. I can reminisce anytime I like without being here.'

CHAPTER TWO

'You won't be living, Caroline; you have to understand you have died.' He spoke with his usual airy calmness, but I raised a challenging eyebrow at him. He let out what I could only describe as the sigh a grandmother gives her misbehaving yet beloved first grandchild. 'So be it, you can change your mind once. Do you genuinely want to leave here?' Michael asked.

'Yes, this isn't right.'

'As *you* wish.' Michael stroked his chin, then rubbed his left ear with his index finger. The girls and my old school melted away.

Chapter Three

We moved again, though not as quickly this time. Instead of a freefall, we floated to the ground like two feathers, and I landed on the sofa in my living room. Michael sat cross-legged beside me.

I scanned the room. It seemed the same as we'd left it. My bright orange candles still stood out against the backdrop of greens and greys which James had insisted on painting the room in. Though not exactly tidy, not one item was out of place.

I shot up and headed to the kitchen, shouting for James as I ran. I could hear Michael yelling my name behind me, but I ignored him. With no indication James had been in the kitchen, I took the stairs two at a time to the bedroom.

He hadn't returned. The house was empty.

'Caroline!' Michael shouted as he reached the top of the stairs. 'I thought you understood that only a living person with a gift can hear you. James isn't here, nor is he gifted. He won't have a clue that you still have a presence in the world. He might have felt a breeze the way you were dashing around, though.' He frowned. 'You shouldn't run so fast in people's houses; you could startle a person. Keep to the corners of the room where possible.'

CHAPTER THREE

'The corners?' I asked, my eyebrows raised.

'Yes, stay in the corners, out of people's way.'

'Michael, there's nobody here.'

'Doesn't matter. Get used to it,' he snapped.

I stepped back and hung my head.

'Sorry,' I mumbled. 'I assume I have a lot to learn?'

'That you do, that you do.' He nodded. 'Bear in mind what I have told you about people's houses, and you won't go far wrong.'

'Okay,' I said, although he hadn't really given me anything useful except to stay in the corners. I paced the floor to avoid his gaze. 'I was hoping that you, Az, and Raff had made a mistake or that I had imagined this whole thing. It's a lot to take in…' I sighed and flopped on the bed. Michael perched beside me.

'I understand, and believe me, you are handling this better than most I've brought back.'

'I think I need clean clothes,' I said, ignoring his attempt to comfort me.

I rose and walked over to my wardrobe; I had rescued it from the council tip and painted the doors a pearlescent blue. One was ajar, and Michael interrupted me as I tried unsuccessfully to pull a t-shirt off its hanger.

'Sorry, Caroline, you've missed the window to change your clothes. I told you once we arrived, you would have the opportunity. You didn't like the first place I took you and then I spent valuable time chasing you all over this *house*.'

I dropped my hands and spun to face him. 'What? That's not fair!'

Michael held my gaze steadily until I stomped my foot and tutted. 'Can I at least change my underwear? I don't want to smell.'

'Not again…' Michael groaned and threw his hands up to the ceiling.

I tilted my head and pursed my lips, wondering what I'd done wrong now. 'What is it?'

'You're not the first person to ask about changing your underwear. Before I brought you back, a woman who died from a heart attack—brought on by laughing too hard, would you believe—had a little accident before she died. She won't smell during her time here, and neither will you. You are dead, *kaput, finis*,' he said flatly.

'Okay, thanks, I get the picture…' I remarked. 'It's awful about that woman, though. What a way to go.'

Michael rolled his eyes. 'Yes, yes, incredibly sad!' He stood up as I sat down. 'Now, if there isn't anything else, I need to go,' he added, then disappeared in a familiar puff of pink smoke.

'Wait!' I shouted, springing from the bed. 'How do I—'

'*Your heart connects you to people, Caroline,*' Michael's voice echoed around the room.

'What the hell does that mean?' I yelled up at the ceiling.

But there was no response.

Great, simply great!

Michael had been incredibly rude, though I suspected he had spent more time with me than he had intended, when I considered how irritable he had become. But still, even if I had gone over my allotted time, a tiny bit of empathy would have gone a long way.

So, there I stood, alone, with no real guidance on account of my lack of questions. I had no clue how to function amongst the living, but before I figured out the ins and outs of this new life, I had a more important task: finding James. My desperation to find him outweighed all the other issues that threatened to flood my mind, and I chose to search the local hospital first.

Before I attempted to leave the house, I looked through the living room window. The sky over our little town still had that grimy film of pollution plastered over it. Cars sped by, not slowing for the numerous speed bumps the community had petitioned so tirelessly for. It had stopped raining long enough for Mr Starr from number sixty-two to walk his terrier, Betsy. *Does he know I died?* I wondered.

Then it hit me; it was still light out. I checked the alarm panel by the front door: half past five. I'd come back the same day. We arrived in the town centre around five o'clock. Thirty minutes had passed since the accident.

As I headed for the front door, I gave my head a wobble and reached for the handle. I wavered, then pushed it down, and the door opened without hesitation. I'd half expected my hand to pass through it like I'd witnessed on TV.

Relief washed over me; I wasn't trapped in the house with no clue how to escape. But I was also perturbed by the action; I knew I'd touched the handle, but I couldn't physically feel it.

I stepped outside and closed the door, then slumped back against it for a moment. I wanted to take a deep breath and release it to expel all the doubts and nerves. It hadn't yet sunk in that I would never breathe again or perform other simple tasks.

My mind formed a list of a hundred and one things now out of reach, but I shook them away and focused on finding James. I closed my eyes for a moment to push everything else away, then proceeded down the path.

The hospital was miles away; it would have been quicker to

cycle, but that was a stupid idea. Can you imagine the looks on people's faces if a bicycle passed by seemingly of its own fruition? I didn't even know if I could still ride a bike.

As I walked, Michael's final words spun around my mind; he said my heart will connect me to people. So I stopped, shut my eyes, and concentrated on my husband—on his eyes, his smile, his touch, his love…

My stomach lurched and flipped.

When I opened my eyes, I found I'd moved from the street to the resuscitation room in the local Accident and Emergency department. James lay unconscious on a trolley in front of me.

Hospital staff hooked him up to a drip and various machines, while others dressed his wounds. I rejoiced he was still alive, though he looked in bad shape with his blackened right eye and bandaged head. He never stirred the entire time.

I overheard a doctor mention they would move him when his condition stabilised. I couldn't ask what his condition was, though the staff didn't intubate him, which I took as a good sign.

Gradually, the doctors and nurses drifted away, and I seized my chance to get closer to him. I placed my hand over his, touching but not feeling his warmth or skin, and I stood watching his chest rise and fall. I listened to the rhythm and beeps of the machines and for any approaching staff.

I don't know how much time passed before a familiar female voice broke my trance.

'James, my love,' the voice uttered on the verge of tears.

At the sound, my head whipped round. If I had been alive, I swear I would have given myself whiplash.

'Clare?' I whispered. 'What are *you* doing here? Why have they let *you* in? You aren't family! "My love"?'

CHAPTER THREE

I removed my hand from James's, and my eyebrows squished together as I tried to process what I'd heard. Clare had only met James once, at our wedding reception.

Hadn't she?

I flinched as she walked to the opposite side of the bed and faced me. She put down her bag, took off her coat, and placed it over the back of a chair, then pulled that chair to his side. Her olive eyes teared up as she sat.

Heavy footsteps marched towards us, and I looked back to find a nurse with a face like thunder.

'Are you a relative?' she asked curtly.

'I'm his girlfriend,' Clare sniffed.

I froze at the sound of the words.

'Two minutes, and you need to leave. He needs his rest,' said the nurse.

Clare nodded.

She tapped something out on her phone while she blinked fast to dispel the tears. Her scarlet nails clicked on the screen as though to taunt me, then she dropped the phone in her bag and took James's hand in hers.

'What are you doing?' I yelled at her as I came to my senses. 'Get your filthy paws off him. He's mine!'

I wanted to launch myself over the bed, grab her, and shake that tiny head off her body. But most of all, I wanted to ask her what right she had to hold *my* husband's hand. Clare was my manager, a person I had respected and considered a friend.

I let out an almighty scream, and a wad of paperwork blew off the table near me. Above, the fluorescent lights flickered, and Clare jumped up off the chair and watched the paperwork scatter to the floor. She glanced at the nearby nurse, who seemed oblivious to what had occurred.

I stretched my neck over the bed. 'That's right, Clare, you better be scared,' I said with as much venom as I could muster.

But none of that made a difference, as she turned to James, stroked his hair, and said, 'It's okay, my love, I'm here. I'll look after you.'

'Oh no, you won't,' I snarled, glancing around for something to throw.

Clare spoke to him like a lover she had known for years, not the husband of a member of her staff. I wanted to puke. I couldn't believe what I'd learned. These two people had betrayed me by having an affair for god knows how long, and now I was dead, she would have him all to herself.

Not if can put an end to it, I thought. I had ten years to kill back here with the living, and I'll be damned if she got to keep him.

Dazed by the revelations, I wandered around A & E, looking for an exit. I didn't know where to go from here, but I knew I had to leave the hospital. I kept a slow pace to avoid people as they went about their day. I wasn't quite ready to find out what would happen if I couldn't evade someone's path.

Eventually, I ended up in a long corridor. I finally found an exit sign, and as I made my way there, I saw a porter looking in my direction from the other end of the corridor.

I checked behind me. I couldn't see anyone else, and as I got closer, he nodded at me. I opened my mouth to speak, but he put his finger to his lips to indicate I should stay silent. I couldn't tell if he was alive or like me.

A group of doctors alighted from a nearby lift; they said their farewells, then scurried off like ants in different directions. I pressed myself as close to the wall as I could to dodge them.

When they had all gone, I looked for the porter, but he had

disappeared with the crowd.

I tutted, gnawing on the inside of my cheek. He could have helped me figure out what I could and couldn't do.

I left the hospital and went to sit in the park to think my options through—what little I had, anyway. I found my favourite bench and took in the familiar surroundings; the sun had started to set, and families were beginning to pack up their picnics. The faint smell of freshly cut grass drifted on the breeze, and the tulips planted by the local council were in full bloom.

I'd been to this park many times to sit and ponder life's hurdles and puzzles. I loved to watch the children and dogs play. They had no cares or worries in the world, and it always calmed my churning mind and brought me back to reality.

Though my reality had changed in a heartbeat; the life I thought I knew was a lie, and my marriage was a sham.

I'd sat here a dozen times, working through problems. I had a lot to work out this time, not a tiny complication; this situation was like conquering Everest when compared. First, I had to figure out what I could do in my new form, whatever I might be: ghost, spirit, or essence. I remembered Raff berated me when I said *ghost*, so I opted for *spirit*.

In a short space of time, I had learnt I could get to places without having to walk, though I wasn't sure how it worked. I had moved objects without touch, and I could open doors. I hoped with every fibre of my being the scare in A & E wasn't a first-time fluke and keeping Clare away would be as easy as pie.

I chewed on my lip as I thought about my new life; the action didn't hurt, which only worried me further. I'd believed I'd be returning to the life I knew, but that was all gone, and that thought only brought new dilemmas.

I wanted revenge, but what would I do after that? Where would I go? I couldn't spend the next ten years terrorising Clare, could I?

Although I knew what I wanted to do, I needed the assistance of a fellow spirit to help me navigate the maze of my new life. I should have asked for a guidebook when I arrived back here. I made a mental note to mention it to Michael when he came back to collect me. I wasn't going to find it sat here, watching the world pass me by.

I glanced up as a woman walked past me; she pushed a pram with one hand while the other hand scrolled through her phone. A little girl dawdled behind her. As they passed, the little girl spoke to me.

'I like your trainers,' she said. 'I've got converse too—pink ones.'

'Wow, that's awesome,' I replied, then muttered, 'What the heck?' once she was out of earshot.

Her mother hadn't noticed our conversation, no doubt too engrossed in whatever travelled across her phone screen. I wondered if her mother knew she had a gifted child, or at least that's what I hoped she was. I couldn't bear to think of the alternative.

As I watched the last of the stragglers leave the park, my stomach started to churn and flip like it had when I moved to the hospital. But this time, an invisible line pulled at me. I couldn't fight the unknown force, so I shut my eyes and waited for where I'd end up next.

The sounds of the park faded away, and I opened my eyes to find I had been pulled into a corridor in an unfamiliar building. A pungent smell filled my nostrils—like bleach, but more robust—and I wondered how anyone could stand working in here without passing out from the fumes. On top of that, I had no idea why I'd been pulled here or who had done it.

Voices mumbled in the distance, so I followed them, thinking they might be responsible.

I walked around a corner and saw the familiar silhouette of my dad. I could spot him anywhere. He had a tuft of brown hair at the back of his head that wouldn't stay down, no matter the volume of gel he lathered on it.

'Dad!' I yelled, forgetting he wouldn't be able to hear me. He was stood between a police officer and a man in a white coat. In front of them was a window with blue curtains pulled shut.

'Are you ready, Mr Johnson?' asked the man in the white coat.

Ready for what?

I stood behind my father as he took a deep breath, then nodded. The man in the white coat pressed a button on the wall, and the curtains opened. I looked over my father's shoulder to see what they were looking at.

Oh, dear god, no!

The window revealed a room with a trolley in the middle. On the stretcher lay a body, draped in a white sheet.

My body.

I understood where I was now, and the reason for the unpleasant smell. A woman beyond the glass lifted the cover to reveal my face as I turned away.

'Mr Johnson?' prompted the police officer.

'Yes, it's my daughter,' he said, stifling a sob.

'I'm sorry for your loss, Mr Johnson,' offered the man in the white coat. 'If you'll follow me, you can collect your daughter's belongings.'

The three men walked away from the window, leaving me to stare at the mound that used to be me. This was proof none of it had been a dream—or a nightmare. The revelation upset me, but I found the tears wouldn't come.

I shouted after them. 'Hey, are you just going to leave me on that dinner trolley?'

With no answer, I chased after my father in the hope my mother would be waiting for him somewhere.

I followed them into a small room, expecting my mother to be sat there, but it was empty except for two plush sofas and a table with my belongings placed on it. I examined the clutter: laid out in plastic bags were a few CDs, a book, and my handbag.

'Oh crap, my handbag!' I said and reached for my side, feeling it there. 'Cool, I've got a spirit handbag. That isn't weird at all…' I frowned.

I hadn't thought about it since I'd tried to call James. It was strange, but also comforting to have something I could hold and touch.

'If you could sign here, Mr Johnson,' said the man in white, giving my father a clipboard and pen. 'Do you have any questions?' he asked while my father sat down and signed the paperwork.

'When can my daughter's body be released?'

'In a few days. You will need to contact a funeral director, and they will liaise with us and guide you through it all.'

'Okay.' He nodded. 'What about the investigation? Do you know what happened?' He turned his attention to the police officer.

'It's still early days, Mr Johnson, but our preliminary investigations and initial witness testimonies suggest your son-in-law

CHAPTER THREE

failed to brake at the lights. There were no tyre marks from their car, indicating he braked too late. It appears to be an unfortunate accident.' The police officer bowed his head, and my father nodded. 'Of course, we will know more when we have looked the car over and spoken with your son-in-law when he wakes up. Do you know if the car has been in the garage recently?'

'I don't know. You'll have to ask James,' my father said sternly.

'We will do that, sir,' the police officer said and scribbled in his notepad.

'Why wouldn't James brake?' I muttered. 'He's the safest driver I know. And no, it hadn't been in the garage. In fact, I think it was due soon. You can't hear me, can you? I'm just stood here, invisible, talking out loud. Shut up, Caroline.' I rolled my eyes at myself.

I hadn't even thought about the accident until then, though I could barely recall what had happened or the events leading up to it.

It can't have been his fault, I thought. Why wouldn't he brake? He didn't have a death wish, did he?

Well, what do I know? I didn't know him at all, apparently.

The men concluded the paperwork, and the police officer walked my father out of the building. I followed him back to his car. He kept a slow step with his head hung low; the bag with my belongings swayed at his side.

How I wished I could reach out and hug him, let him feel my presence.

My mother was nowhere to be seen, no doubt too upset to make the journey with him. I remembered I'd reached James by closing my eyes and focusing on him, so I did the same with my mother. I felt the familiar sensation of my stomach churning, then opened my eyes, finding myself outside their cottage in the lake district.

Okay, so I hadn't got as close as I had with James, but at least I knew how to get to someone, now.

I'd always dreamt of packing up and moving away to the country in my golden years, and I had envied my parents so much when my father retired early. They packed up and moved to the beautiful town of Grasmere where they'd bought two run-down cottages: one to live in and the other to use as a holiday let. They often let us stay in the holiday let—out of peak season, of course. Still, I loved it here; it was the perfect place to get away from our busy lives.

I dashed through the little wooden gate and ran around the back of the cottage to the kitchen door, where I lifted the latch and crept inside.

The sweet tobacco smoke of my dad's pipe lingered in the air.

I went through to the sitting room, which was as I remembered from our last visit; the chessboard sat on the coffee table, frozen midway through our previous match (my father and I played for hours, much to the annoyance of my mother and husband); an unread copy of *Country Living* sat beside it—my mother never read them, yet she refused to cancel the subscription. I suspected she wanted to fit in with the neighbours when they called round; and the Royal Dalton tea set I bought for them rested on its silver serving tray, still unused through my mother's fear of breaking it.

I crept upstairs to her bedroom and found her fast asleep. On the bedside table stood a bottle of Valium. I assumed my father had retrieved it from the back of the medicine cabinet when they heard the news.

My mother had always struggled with a nervous disposition, but since moving to the country, she had really kept her anxiety under control without the need for medication, and I was so proud of her for getting better.

I crouched down and studied her face; she looked peaceful, far away from the horror that faced her when she woke up.

The landline started ringing, and my mother stirred. 'Caroline,' she whispered softly.

'I'm here, Mum.' I placed my hand over hers, and she fell back to sleep.

I sat in that position until my father arrived home. I heard his heavy steps on the stairs, then he tiptoed into the bedroom and switched on the bedside lamp. His eyes were rimmed red, and his nose was sore; he appeared to have cried all the way home.

He gently touched my mother's face, then crept back downstairs as the phone rang again. My mother didn't stir this time. I followed him back to the sitting room, where he picked up the phone and slammed it down. Then he disconnected the line.

He sat in his favourite chair and sighed heavily. For a moment, all was quiet. I sat beside him, and both of our gazes rested on the chessboard. In a flash, he got up with such force, the chair moved backwards, and he swiped the chess pieces from the board, scattering them across the room.

I wanted so badly to go over to my father and embrace him, tell him everything would be fine, that I was bewildered but okay, and that I would watch over him until I moved on. Moved on—when I would be taken from the world once again.

What am I going to do? my brain shouted over and over and

over.

I thought seeing my parents would help me—guide me, somehow, so I could be at peace with what had happened and plan for the time I would spend here. I had ten years to come to terms with my early demise, but really, I hadn't a clue what I was going to do with myself.

My father didn't move from that chair all night. He dozed now and again, until my mother came down in the morning. Her flowing caramel hair had lost its usual shine, and her face looked tired and gaunt, as if she had aged twenty years overnight.

'Tell me it isn't true, Bob. Tell me it's all been a dream. A nightmare,' she said, her voice straining to hold back sobs.

My father sighed. 'I wish I could, Marge, I really do.'

He got up and joined her on the sofa. He rocked her gently and stroked her back as she wept.

All I could do was watch in horror.

Minutes and hours blurred together as I watched my parents in their darkest of days. I quickly established that us spirits don't need to sleep, eat, or drink, or do anything like we used to. The remnants of my bodily functions had faded away like Az said they would, and my senses remained intact, though my emotions seemed off.

My father busied himself with phone calls and making arrangements. I listened from the back of the room to his first conversation.

'Good morning, Father…'

'Yes, Father, we will arrange for a funeral director to collect her and bring her here…'

'I don't care about her husband!' my father snarled.

'Sorry, Father.'

CHAPTER THREE

'Yes, Father, I'll be in touch.'

I couldn't listen to anymore. I didn't want to know what my funeral arrangements would be.

I gave my father's shoulder a squeeze, then left the room.

I found my mother in the kitchen poring over old photos of me, an array of tear-stained tissues crowding any available space. I'd seen them shed lots of tears, though not a single one would fall from my eyes. Not for me and not for them.

I knelt beside her and put my hand on her knee. Her weeping subsided into gentle sobs, then tiny hiccups.

My mother had always taken pictures of me on my first day of term and the last day, every year until I left for university. She had complied them and given them to me on my twenty-first birthday, and she'd kept copies for herself, too.

It was this album that she was looking at when she shouted for my father.

'Bob, would you come in here?' she shouted from the kitchen. 'Bob, are you listening to me?'

My father shuffled in. 'What is it, Marge?'

'Come sit with me a moment, dear. There's fresh tea in the pot.'

I laughed. The teapot had a chip in it. I wished she would use the set I'd given her now more than ever.

My father poured himself a cup and added two heaps of sugar.

My mother tutted. 'Bob, you promised you'd cut down. Think about your cholesterol.'

'I have cut down. I used to have four,' he chuckled.

'I'm sure what you've just spooned in was the equivalent of four.' She laughed too.

The sound of their laughter warmed my heart, and I smiled

from ear to ear.

'Look at our little girl…' said my mother, circling my young face with her finger.

'Yes, I see,' my father said, then slurped his tea.

'She loved that doll.'

'I remember. She took it everywhere.'

I peered at the picture; my seven-year-old self gazed back at me. I was holding a Bratz doll. Now I knew where I got my dress sense from.

They continued to flip through the album until they reached my final year of secondary school.

'Doesn't it seem like yesterday when she was getting ready for her final year?' asked my mother, and my father nodded.

'You have no idea, Mum. I was there five minutes ago. What a nightmare.'

I embraced both my parents as they reminisced over my school days. I could tell my presence was having a positive effect on them, as the sadness receded and tears dried over the time I spent with them.

After a couple of days, people started to stop by. I studied the faces of the neighbours who came to share in my parents' grief, despite never having met me. They sat and smiled as my mother retrieved the album again.

I was touched at how loved and supported they were, despite being reasonably new to the area. I sat and held my mother's hand as she told stories about me to anyone who would listen.

Sunday came, my parents wedding anniversary (though neither acknowledged it), and I had been a spirit for nearly a week. It was a quarter to one in the morning, and I was sat with my father in the kitchen—evidently, he couldn't sleep. He was sorting through all the casseroles and desserts people had brought by. I hadn't realised people still brought food after a bereavement. *It must be a country thing*, I reasoned with myself.

My mother had been in bed for hours, exhausted from the day's flurry of visitors. I went upstairs and lay next to her. I had a spiritual instinct to provide comfort to her, to see if she could feel my presence as I suspected. I nuzzled into her back like I had when I was a child and put my arm over her. Moments passed, then she sighed softly.

The bedroom door creaked open, and my father shuffled inside. I slid off the bed and sat on the floor in the corner.

'Is that you, Bob?' my mother whispered.

'Who else would it be, dear? Your secret toy boy?' he laughed.

I couldn't see my mother's face, but I knew she must have smiled. My father always knew how to cheer her up.

'How are you feeling? Have you been asleep?'

'Yes, I've napped a little here and there. Have you left the heating on? I'm sweltering.' She wafted the sheets up and down around her.

'No, dear, but you do feel a bit warm. Would you like a glass of water?'

'Yes, please, dear.'

At this point, my intuition told me my parents would survive the horror of my death. I was so sure of it that I made the choice to leave them when they rose in the morning. I needed to be on my own for a while, far away from the people I knew and loved.

I would head for the beach in Saint Bees. My parents had taken me there often as a child, and I knew it wasn't far. Considering I could no longer get tired or complain about my feet aching, I knew I could make it by the afternoon. I wanted to sit on the sand, listen to the waves softly crashing on the shore, and allow the sea air to fill my nostrils.

I watched my parents from my little spot in the corner of their bedroom. There, they enjoyed a restful sleep for the first time in days. And as that dreaded day arrived again—Monday, one week since the accident—the sun rose and shone brightly over their house.

I left then, knowing in my soul that they would survive this and continue to live their lives to the fullest without their little girl.

Chapter Four

At my parents' home, I'd had a lot of time to think, and my thoughts would often turn to James and Clare. A fire raged within me for what they had done behind my back, yet despite the betrayal, a hint of love lingered in my heart for him.

Clare was another matter entirely; visions filled my head of different ways I could hurt her. My favourite one had me marching into the office and punching her full in the face in front of everyone.

Regardless of how entertaining the ideas were, they all involved actions I could no longer perform. I needed a realistic solution to force her to leave him alone, but before that, I had to find someone to help me.

I walked through Grasmere with purpose in my stride, my direction set on the beach. I hoped the walk would give me time to shake away the last bit of love I had for my husband and the echoes of the policeman's voice who reminded me James had failed to brake.

I hated the Monday morning rush; people ran to catch buses, early risers finished their morning jogs, and a young mother yelled at her son to pick up his packed lunch that he had decided to empty out onto the floor in a tantrum.

I dodged pedestrians and flirted with danger on my unknown path. I no longer waited patiently for cars to pass; I crossed last minute when I wanted to. The three drain covers in a row that I used to avoid due to my friend's superstition were now a game; I played hopscotch on them and laughed like a child again.

Tamara always told me not to walk on them, as she believed they brought bad luck. I remembered on one occasion, we were happily walking down the high street, and out of nowhere, she pushed me into the path of three men dressed in suits. Of course, I had been mortified and apologised profusely, my face turning scarlet as I spoke.

'What was that about?' I had asked as we continued on our way.

She laughed cheekily. 'Oh, you nearly walked over three drains.'

I knew she had lied on that occasion; Tamara had tried all sorts to set me up with a man until I met James. I reminded her several times that what worked for her wouldn't necessarily work for me—the right guy would come my way when the time was right.

Tamara was spontaneous and up to go on any sort of date; fishing, paragliding, you name it, she's done it. And she could talk to anyone. None of that was me.

It made me wonder if my personality had been the reason for the affair.

I quickly switched my mind from those thoughts and back to my friends. I promised myself I would visit them all once I had a strategy in place to deal with Clare.

As I walked, I pondered why I couldn't make a distinction between the living and the dead. If everyone had the option to come back, then there had to be other spirits somewhere. So perhaps not everyone had the chance to come back—only a few were selected, due to overcrowding. I wondered why they'd picked me, then. It wasn't as though I'd done anything special with my life.

Before long, I had made my way to Hardknott Pass. I amazed myself. I'd reached my destination without the need for a map or directions. It made me wonder if spirits had a sixth sense for travel. And I didn't feel tired, not one bit. I had run, skipped, and jumped all the way here. It pleased me to know I could go where I wanted on a whim, no matter how far, as my feet would no longer pound to their own beat, begging for a rest.

I ran the rest of the way to Saint Bees. My new nimble form dodged dog walkers and ramblers alike as I whizzed along uneven paths. I felt more alive than ever! A sense of freeness hung over me, and I fought the urge to yell, 'Catch me if you can, suckers!' As good as it felt in the moment, I sensed it to be wrong, somehow.

I struggled to comprehend that only a week ago I had succumbed to an untimely end, but I'd never felt so unrestricted to do as I pleased, instead of putting others first.

I half expected I would have been maudlin for the next ten years, stood in a corner, having conversations with dust bunnies. Perhaps that's what others did; played by the rules, not leaving their old houses, sticking to the corners...

Nevertheless, the sensation stayed with me. Though I noticed one thing as I ran and frolicked by myself: I could no longer feel the warmth of the sun on my face.

I'd always liked to have a bit of colour on my skin—though, not as much as those people whose skin resembled that of an old leather handbag. I did try self-tanning products once, but

I ended up looking like a tangerine.

I skipped merrily towards the promenade, glad to find I could smell the sea air and hear the waves. There weren't many people this end of the beach. A couple of Labradors chased sticks on the sand, which I was sure wasn't allowed. An older couple strolled hand in hand and without a care in the world by the smiles on their faces.

I smiled at them, then took my first step onto the beach.

A voice yelled in the distance. I took my foot off the sand and glanced around for the owner.

A man ran towards me in an army parka that billowed behind him as he moved. He pointed and waved at the sea, his arms all over the place as he yelled at me to stop, over and over.

Without hesitation, I walked over to him; a deed I would never have done before.

'You can't go on the beach in your condition,' he said with a bony finger jabbed at me.

'You can see me!' I said, punching the air. 'At last, someone can see me.'

'Of course, I can see you; don't talk wet.'

I ignored the ancient phrase my gran used to use. I couldn't insult the first person to have a conversation with me in days.

'Sorry if I seem clueless. I'm new to all this, and you're the first person I've spoken to since I died.' I paused, expecting him to say something. Instead, he fiddled with a toggle on his coat. 'It's been an awfully long week…' I continued. 'How did you know I was dead?'

'Many years of experience,' he said curtly.

'Why can't I go on the beach?'

'Well, I don't have time to go into all the particulars, but the sea is magnetised. Once you're in spirit form, the sea pulls you

CHAPTER FOUR

in like a giant magnet. If you had got within ten metres of the sea, you would have been pulled off the edge of the Earth to who knows where.' He shrugged as though this was something I should know. 'For some reason, newbies are always drawn to the beach, and it's my job to stop you lot from going near the sea.'

I cocked my head. 'Really? This is your job?'

'Yes, really. This is my profession on God's green earth. Go ahead, see for yourself, if you don't believe me.' He stepped to the side as he spoke.

I studied him for a moment. His mousy-brown hair fell in thick curtains, framing both sides of his face, and he was about two days overdue a shave.

Now I had two options: one, write him off as crazy and take the chance I wouldn't be pulled off the Earth by an unknown entity, or two, believe every word he said and perhaps he would help me out.

His parka was adorned with little badges and pins. I focused on a tiny, blue peace symbol; I took that as a sign I should believe him.

'I think I'll stay put. Thank you for saving me,' I said.

'No thanks necessary, all part of the service.'

'Is this all you do all day?'

'Yep, I've got nothing better to do. This is my *happy place*,' he said, using air quotes. 'And I like my job.'

'Oh, I see.' I wasn't entirely convinced he enjoyed standing out here all day. 'Well, do you think you could help me?'

'Help you with what?' he said, distracted as he looked over the top of my head.

I glanced over my shoulder but couldn't see what he was looking at.

'Well, what can I do?' I asked. 'How can I spot others like us? What are we called? Can I scare some—'

'Woah, slow down,' he said, holding his hands up. 'One question at a time. I can answer a couple of your questions, but I'm not really the best person to ask. I haven't spent that much time with others, learning how to develop my skills, but perhaps I can point you in the right direction. You'll probably benefit from the assistance of a mentor. First things first, though—if we are going to converse some more, I should at least know your name.'

'I'm Caroline.'

In any other circumstance, I would have extended my hand to shake his as I would with anyone I met for the first time. But this time, I thought better of it; what if we couldn't touch each other and my hand went straight through his?

He nodded. 'I'm Daniel. Now, to answer your first question, you can do lots of things, but it takes patience and practice. Have you moved anything yet?'

'Yes, I saw my husband in the hospital—'

'Let me guess,' he cut in, 'you were angry at something?'

'Yes, he'd been—'

'Shush! Don't interrupt me.' I frowned at his rudeness, as he had interrupted me first, but he added, 'And don't pout, it doesn't suit your pretty face.'

I smiled.

'So...'

'Wait,' he said. He itched his right arm, then looked around, perplexed, then he ran back the way he had come from.

'Hang on!' I chased after him.

Daniel ran down the promenade, then skidded to an abrupt halt. I heard a loud whoosh, then a woman screamed.

CHAPTER FOUR

'That was your fault.' He spun to point at me as I stopped behind him. 'You and your incessant questions have made me lose someone.'

'I'm sorry, I didn't mean to distract you from your work. I was just excited to meet you,' I said. Maybe he *had* told me the truth about the sea.

'They've been dragged off the edge of the Earth through no fault of their own,' he said stroking the nape of his neck.

'I am truly sorry,' I said, trying to sound as sincere as I could. 'But can I ask another question? What do you mean by "the edge of the Earth"? You've said it twice now. The Earth is round; there is no edge.' I instantly regretted asking when I watched his face drop.

He folded his arms. 'Well, *that's* where you're wrong!' he sang. 'I don't know what BS your teachers fed you at school, but the Earth is flat; it has an edge.'

Brilliant, I thought. The first spirit I was interacting with was a Flat Earther. Just my luck, I meet an escapee from the mental asylum.

'Umm...' I hesitated.

I couldn't think of a suitable response. At this point, I thought Daniel had lost the plot, but I needed his help, no matter his kooky explanations and beliefs.

'Listen here...' He moved closer to me so he could whisper, though there was no one remotely close to us. 'NASA is nothing more than a government conspiracy machine. They fill your heads with the information they want you to believe; they don't want you to know the truth.' He stopped to look over his shoulder. 'Just look at the supposed moon landing. If you look at Neil Armstrong's boots, they don't even match the footprints on the surface of the moon.'

I snorted. 'Okay, calm down, Fox Mulder,' I teased.

'Who's this Fox Mulder?' he said, expressionless. 'I told you, my name's Daniel.'

'*The X-Files?*' I prompted, but his face remained blank. 'Big TV show. Full of conspiracy theories…' I added, but he continued to stare at me. 'You've never heard of *The X Files?*'

Daniel shook his head.

'Daniel, when did you die?' I asked, eyeing his clothes again. He wore Fred Perry and Lambretta pin badges, reminding me of an extra from that *scooter* film—I forget what it's called.

'1984.'

'Oh, well, that explains it. The show came out in the nineties; you would have loved it. Anyway,' I changed the subject, 'you've been a spirit for a long time, you must have a few tricks up your sleeve.' I glanced to my left and saw the older couple I'd spotted earlier; they were now carrying ice-creams. The smell of mint-choc-chip mixed with the salty air reminded me of the previous summer when Tamara and I had taken her daughter, Eliza, to the beach for the first time.

'I know a few things, but I already told you, I haven't spent that much time with others like us. To move something, you must tune in to your emotions,' he said pointing to his head. 'You can travel wherever you like,' he continued. 'Although, it's easier if you know someone in the location you want to go, as you have a connection. If you've never been somewhere, you have to concentrate hard on where you want to go, or you could end up any old place,' he said, leaning to his right to look past me once more. I looked over my shoulder but, yet again, couldn't see what he was looking at.

I shook my head a little to remove the paranoia that seemed to be rubbing onto me from Daniel.

CHAPTER FOUR

'Let me see if I have this correct,' I said, ignoring how distracted he was. 'I can think of any place in the world, and I'll be there. In the same way I thought of my husband and mother, then I was with them.'

'Yes, in theory, though it's not as easy as it sounds. You'll have to practice. You'll no doubt get it wrong the first few times. Best place to be is in the open, if you ask me,' he said, gesturing to the wide-open space we stood in. 'Oh, and above all, remember not to draw attention to yourself.'

'What if I want to draw attention to myself?' I asked, testing the words.

He hummed, eyeing me dubiously. 'It is possible, although a taboo area. I don't get involved with that chicken shittery, and you shouldn't, either. Please excuse my language. It's a fool's game. But it can be done,' Daniel said, stroking his stubble. 'You should go see Frankie G in London. He has a pub where spirits meet up and chat. I'm sure you'll find it enlightening, and you'll find someone to help you there.'

'What pub?'

'Er…' He glanced at the sea where the waves had become loud and choppy, then looked down the beach for the umpteenth time. 'The Lion's Head? Yes, that's one. Get yourself off now. I've got work to do; I can't be losing anyone else today.'

'Okay,' I mumbled, trying to hide my disappointment. 'Before I go, how many years did you get?'

'Why does that matter? It's all relative, anyway.'

'Right…' I said, wondering what the hell that meant.

'Good luck, Caroline!' Daniel shouted as he ran off down the promenade.

Chapter Five

I watched Daniel resume his lookout position. He scanned around and looked at me longer than he needed to.

Meeting Daniel had been interesting, to say the least. Perhaps he had not been the best person to get help from, but he had saved me, if I was to believe his weird theories. I had to admit, at the start, I hadn't been totally convinced, though I had heard something strange, and the female scream had been odd too.

I couldn't stay here. Even after our conversation, the beach still tempted me, and I didn't know how long I'd be able to fight the urge to step onto it.

What Daniel had told me swam around my head. Armed with the information he had given me, I decided it would be best to go home to familiar surroundings to plan my next steps.

I concentrated hard on the times spent with James in our home. The familiar sensation of being pulled washed over me, and I shut my eyes. When I opened them, I had travelled away from the beach, but I hadn't arrived home. I'd landed in someone else's living room.

'Oh, shoot...' I muttered.

I had no idea where I'd transported myself. The room had hardly any furniture; a sofa and TV were all that had been placed there. An oversized clock hung at a crooked angle on the wall, showing the time to be three o'clock. It had taken me longer to get to Saint Bees than I'd thought.

I looked around. The kitchen had a fridge but no other white appliances—only gaping black holes where they should have been. I looked for the bedroom. It appeared to be an apartment, as there were no stairs. The bedroom had a bed and one bedside cabinet with a picture of a couple on it.

I turned to leave, but curiosity made me take a second look at the picture. I moved closer as I recognised the man and the woman he embraced.

James and Clare were laughing at me.

I clenched my fists and screamed. The wooden bed frame rattled and shook with my anger. As I calmed, the bed stilled, though it had moved two feet away from the wall. How naïve I had been. All the signs were there: the late nights, the disappearing money, the texts from CJ. James had felt guilty which explained the spontaneous gifts, and I had been too blind to see it.

My so-called husband and Clare had themselves a little love nest. Why they didn't go to her house was beyond me. Her place was bigger than ours, although I'd only ever hovered on the doorstep. God knows what this hovel was costing.

I could picture it in my mind, them laughing behind my back as they cuddled on the sofa and made love under those horrid red silk sheets. And the next morning, she would waltz into work and have the audacity to ask me about my evening, knowing full well I'd spent it alone.

I shuffled back to the living room and sank onto the sofa.

At least I knew the extent of the affair, despite how much it pained me. Neither of them could be innocent in this catastrophe, but I had to make Clare pay. James had already had his comeuppance; he'd lost me, and he might not wake up from his coma.

Daniel said I should go to The Lion's Head in London and speak to Frankie G. I hoped there wasn't more than one pub with that name, or I could be hopping all over London.

I forgot about going home and closed my eyes, thinking about the pub instead. I tried to envisage what it might look like on the outside, in the hope I would get it right the first time.

I seemed to be floating for ages before I landed, and I knew wherever I had gone was sunny, as the backs of my eyelids were now bright red. I opened one eye slowly, then the other.

I hadn't arrived at the pub. Somehow, I'd landed in a zoo, outside a lion's enclosure, and I was quite sure I'd travelled outside the UK. In fact, it sounded like I'd landed somewhere in the United States if the accents around me were anything to go by.

'Great, just great!' I yelled to the throngs of people around me.

'I'd move away from there, if I were you, ma'am,' said a woman with a southern drawl.

I peered over my shoulder. A woman stood behind me, hands on her hips and dressed in a khaki shirt, shorts, and walking boots. Her sun-kissed skin almost sparkled, and her dark roots peeked through, indicating she was not a natural blonde.

'You can see me?' I enquired, moving away from the enclosure.

'Yes, ma'am.'

'Are you like me? A spirit, I mean.'

'Yes, ma'am. You're British,' she observed. 'What'cha doing here?'

'Good question. I think I got lost,' I said, looking at the people milling around dressed in t-shirts and shorts and carrying maps larger than their bodies. Cameras flashed around me, and I briefly wondered how I would appear in photographs; as a shadow or perhaps an orb?

'I'll say,' said the woman, drawing my attention back to her.

'Where am I?'

'Alabama, ma'am.'

'Woah, I missed by a long way…' I whispered. 'Out of interest, why did you tell me to move away from the enclosure?'

'Oh, the cats can sense beings like us. Don't want them getting all riled up now. Scares the visitors.'

I nodded several times, as though the action would help me absorb what she'd told me.

'I best be getting on, ma'am,' she said and spun around, her ponytail swinging wildly.

'Hang on, wait a minute, please!' I shouted after her. I wanted to ask her what she had to do. After all, she was a spirit like me. I couldn't be sure if she had a specific like Daniel. Though I suspected Daniel only watched out for others to pass the time, not because he had to.

'Yes, ma'am?'

'Do you have a job here?' I asked.

'Yes, ma'am. I tend to the animals when the keepers leave for the day.'

How can that be possible? I wondered, though I didn't ask. Instead, I asked, 'Do all spirits have jobs?'

Her eyebrows knitted together. 'Well, I believe they do, ma'am. Though not many come by the zoo. You're the first

I've seen in months.'

'Have you been outside the zoo?'

'No, ma'am. I like it here. The zoo was my life,' she said, looking around.

I frowned. 'Okay... Thank you.'

'Have a nice day, ma'am.' She waved and left.

'Yes, you too...' I trailed off.

I dodged the crowds of people and found an empty bench to sit on. I was baffled. I'd travelled to the other side of the world in search of a pub and met a spirit who had resumed her previous job at the zoo as though nothing had happened.

It made no sense.

I thought it would be easy to get where I wanted, like it had been with my parents' house and James.

Determination tore through me, and I tried again, telling myself not to overthink it. I closed my eyes and thought of the pub for a second time. After a tug and a pull, I arrived in a new place to the sound of heavy traffic and water, as though I'd landed near a fountain.

I opened my eyes to be met by a statue of a lion. When I looked up, I saw Nelson's Column. I had never been to London before, but I recognised the landmark. I'd made it to London, but instead of the pub, I'd travelled to Trafalgar Square. I told myself this attempt was better than the zoo; at least I'd made it to the right city.

Not wanting to hang around, I pushed through the annoyance and tried again, hoping it would be third-time lucky. This time, I kept my eyes open, and I made it.

In front of me stood The Lion's Head. Not a large pub, but it still had a massive set of wooden double doors. I pulled my shoulders back, held my head up high, and went in.

CHAPTER FIVE

The stench of stale ale hit me, and oddly, I could smell old tobacco, though the smoking ban had been in place for many years. People were having conversations, and the jukebox played Johnny Cash's *Ring of Fire*.

I headed towards the voices, despite not knowing if they were spirits or the living. The pub had a small stage with a stool and microphone stand on it. At least a dozen people sat around in little groups, chatting away. I had to be brave now; I never liked talking to crowds of people. I'd only just managed to get my embarrassment under control at work.

Biting the bullet, I shouted, 'Hello, can anyone hear me?'

A couple of people turned to look at me.

'I'm looking for Frankie G?' I said with confidence, though I couldn't stop playing with the clasp on my handbag.

A middle-aged woman who bore a striking resemblance to a garden gnome and wore horn-rimmed glasses pointed towards a booth in the corner and went back to her conversation.

I marched towards the table; four men sat there, deep in discussion. In my old life, I would never have approached a table full of men. I had never even asked a man for his phone number. But since I'd died, I had found my confidence grew a little with each obstacle I faced.

'Excuse me, gentlemen,' I said, flicking my hair for good measure.

No one spoke, but they all stared. I instantly regretted putting on a front. I'm sure they saw straight through the façade.

'I'm looking for Frankie G...' I mumbled.

The men continued to gawk at me. I'd never felt so insecure. I wanted Michael to collect me right then and there to save me from the humiliation.

'I met this guy on the beach; he said I should come here,' I added.

'What guy?' asked one of the men.

Relief washed over me. I turned to face the man who had spoken. He wore a double-breasted pinstripe suit and a trilby hat. He looked like he had fallen right out the pages of *The Great Gatsby*.

'Daniel. I met him at Saint Bees.'

'That stupid fuck,' he said through clenched teeth. He leant back in the booth, then continued: 'I'm sorry, doll face, but this is an exclusive joint; invitation only.'

Doll face?

'But—'

'But *nothing*, sweetheart. You gotta leave. Now.' He nodded towards the door.

I had come this far, I couldn't let him put me off. I'd seen enough movies to know he was the monkey and not the organ-grinder.

'I'm not leaving until I speak to the boss, not his sidekick,' I said with venom.

The other three men burst into fits of laughter and banged their fists on the table. If looks could kill, I'd be dead twice over with the daggers Gatsby threw at me.

'Knock it off, lads,' said a voice behind me. He spoke with a thick cockney accent. 'Move aside and make room for the lady.'

The men shuffled round to make room, and I sat down, trying not to look smug.

'I'm Frankie G,' said the man as he sat opposite me.

'I'm Caroline, I died a week ago. I met a man called Daniel, and he said I should come to see you. That I'd be able to learn

CHAPTER FIVE

here.'

'Hmm, did he now? That son of a gun.'

I nodded, but my confidence had started to wane. I felt uncomfortable surrounded by all these men. I could feel their eyes on me, sizing me up. However, I found I wasn't blushing for the first time in my existence.

Frankie G ran a large hand over his bald head as he pondered my statement. He wore a polo-neck jumper, blue jeans, and a Harrington jacket. I got the distinct impression Daniel shouldn't be giving away this location to all and sundry.

'Dead a week, you say? You've learnt how to get here quick enough. What have you come here for, exactly?' he asked.

I hadn't expected to be confronted with this question. My main plan involved Clare. I hadn't thought much past what I would do after that. I supposed having some friends wouldn't be a bad thing.

'Well, I'll start from the beginning,' I said. 'I decided to come back so I could watch over my husband and parents. Not long after I returned, I found out my husband has been having an affair with my manager. I want revenge. Daniel told me this was the best place to come to learn and talk with others. Also, I've got ten years to spend here, and it would be nice to spend time with others.'

'Hmm, Daniel, yes, I remember him... What conspiracy theory is he banging on about now? Elvis? JFK? Reptilian elites?' He smirked.

'Flat Earth and the moon landing,' I said innocently.

The group roared with laughter again.

'That old chestnut,' Frankie said between laughs. 'Be honest with me, Caroline, why are you really here?'

Revenge, revenge, revenge.

'Firstly, I need to learn how to get revenge. Secondly, I don't want to be on my own. I've visited my parents, and... I don't think they need me to watch out for them.' I looked down at the table.

I felt some of the men shift uncomfortably. I sensed they weren't used to women sharing their feelings.

'This is what this place is about,' Frankie said, opening his arms. 'Being open, honest, spending time with others, and above all, you can learn things. Though I don't condone hurting the living, mind. You are free to come and go as you please. But obviously, we have nothing happening between eleven in the morning and midnight—to avoid the punters, you know?'

I nodded. 'Sure, great, thank you so much. But why do you let some spirits in now? It's four o'clock.' I hoped I hadn't overstepped.

'VIPs whom I trust not to interfere with the living. I like you, Caroline, you have guts standing up to Jack like that.' He paused to scan the room. 'I'll tell you what, be here in the morning at one, and I'll have one of my regulars meet you, talk you through a few things. How does that sound?'

'Sounds good to me. Sorry, I have one more question: how can I tell the time? I never wore a watch when I was alive, and I don't want to keep going home to look at a clock.'

'You're in London now, baby, Big Ben is not far from here. Have you never been to London?' he said, folding his arms on the table. I noticed a huge, gold knuckle duster on three of his fingers. My eyes fell to my hands folded in my lap, and I tried to remove my wedding band.

'No, this is my first time...' I said, distracted by the ring that wouldn't budge.

CHAPTER FIVE

'Well, have a look around and have fun.' Frankie winked.

'Okay, I'll try,' I said and got up from the table to leave.

'And, sweetheart, leave by the back door, will you? Remember the golden rule,' he said.

I looked at them, puzzled.

'Don't draw attention to yourself,' all the men sang together.

'Oops, sorry,' I said, remembering I had come in through the front door.

I took that as my cue to leave. I left through the back door and exited into an alley. The alley was gloomy despite it being the afternoon, and it stank of vomit and piss. There were too many dark corners, and dustbins for people to hide in for my liking.

Nothing to be scared of, I told myself over and over as I walked along, trying to get to the main road. A scuffling behind some bins made me jump, and I hurried along faster.

Just rats, just rats, I said in my head.

I passed a homeless man asleep on a dirty mattress with all his worldly belongings in a plastic carrier bag. I expected I would see more sights like this in London. It depressed me that in this day and age, not everyone had a place to call home. I couldn't even offer to buy him a coffee or a sandwich.

I eventually emerged onto a little side street. I turned around a full 360 degrees to see if I could spot Big Ben towering over London. I couldn't see it, even though Frankie G had said it wasn't far away.

I carried on walking until I hit the main road. It had become much busier with black cabs and buses full of commuters on their way home. And it was loud. I had never heard the noise of so much traffic before; it certainly wasn't like this up North.

Bikes weaved in and out of the cars, people honked their

horns (seemingly for no reason), and I struggled to make my way through the streams of people heading for home in different directions. I knew at some point I wouldn't be able to get through the throes of people, and my path would cross with someone.

Straight ahead, a young couple were heading my way. I stood still, braced myself, and waited for what would happen next. The woman walked right through me, bringing with her an intense heat. As fast as the phenomenon came, it went.

'Oh! Someone just walked over my grave,' said the woman as she shivered.

It made me think of all the times I had felt a shiver down my spine and used the same expression. I must have walked through a few spirits in my life. It was odd that I had felt heat; perhaps the encounter forced a transfer of energy.

I decided I would walk my own path from then on, instead of zigzagging around people. I wasn't hurting anyone. If anyone felt a shiver for a few seconds, it wasn't going to be detrimental to their lives.

I walked around for a while. I'd never seen the appeal of London before; daily news reports were constantly filled with the horrors of yet another teen stabbing in our nation's capital. I was of the opinion that violence breeds violence. Did nobody ever think that the news reports made it worse, and crime is sensationalised?

It wasn't nice to think I was only safe walking the streets because I no longer lived. Or at least I hoped I was safe. I still had a lot to learn.

Finally, I could see Big Ben; the face showed a quarter past four. To be honest the concept of time no longer mattered to me, only the 3645 days I had left.

Chapter Six

I had some time to kill before I returned to The Lion's Head. Apprehension threatened to engulf my return visit, as I didn't know what to expect. I thought it would be best to take my mind off it by being a tourist for the day. The bonus of my spirit form meant I could skip the queues, and I didn't have to pay.

The walk through London soothed me, mainly because the weather no longer bothered me; it could rain, sleet, turn hot or cold, and it wouldn't affect or hinder me. It might seem strange, but I enjoyed the freedom my new life brought me.

When I told Michael that he'd taken me to the wrong time and place, I'd experienced a shadow of doubt. Now, as I walked past Sir Winston Churchill's statue, I'd never been so sure that I'd opted for the right path.

Although I'd never felt the need to visit London before, Buckingham Palace was my first point of call. And despite it being home to the world's longest reigning monarch, it didn't enthral me like I thought it should. I expected bells, whistles, and grandeur. Instead, I thought it had a lot of hype; film and television made it seem majestic and mysterious, when in real life, even the Queen's guards looked bored.

It reminded me of when James and I went to Rome for our

honeymoon. We'd decided to walk to Vatican City. One of my teachers had been a nun for twenty years before turning her hand to teaching; she always piped on about how it should be a must-visit for all Catholics and non-Catholics alike.

James had to navigate us through ticket touts and people selling bracelets and knockoffs. He held me tight for fear of losing me in the crowds which resembled a packed can of sardines. When we emerged from the sea of people, I'll always remember James uttering 'Is that it?'

I'd echoed his sentiments in my own thoughts; it didn't appear special or sacred to me. James huffed and rambled on about how the church had become a money-making machine as we trundled off to look for the Trevi Fountain.

I sighed as I took one last glance at the palace, then I trudged towards Knightsbridge. The disappointment from my first stop fluttered away as I passed Harrods. I saw signs for the Natural History Museum as I continued, and I made a note to go back there another day.

I spent a good hour with my nose pressed up against shop windows as I drooled over expensive clothes and shoes. But I moved on when I spotted a strange shadow forming in the reflection. My head spun round and whatever it was disappeared.

As shops made way for houses, I entertained myself by looking through sitting room windows where I could, scrutinising the décor and guessing the occupants' professions based on their furniture. I only spent a few minutes at each house, though, for fear of another spirit catching me and accusing me of voyeurism. Which was strange, as I sensed somebody was watching me.

I took a moment to pause on the footpath before I moved to

the next home, but yet again, nothing presented itself. Perhaps Daniel's paranoia really had got to me.

I sighed and moved on with a shake of my head. Couples cooked dinner together, kids watched cartoons on TV, and teenagers fiddled with their phones. I would no longer do anything I witnessed.

I missed my first cup of coffee in the morning, the taste of steak melting on my tongue, even the chime of an incoming email.

Boredom soon set in, and I started the long walk to the East End.

I knew I'd changed postcodes as high-end shops became pound shops and kebab huts. I thought I saw the same shadow in another window and so I crossed the road to avoid whatever it was and dived into a charity shop. I loved charity shops; you would be surprised at the bargains to be had, hidden away on shelves and racks.

A teenage girl with more piercings than I could count sat behind the counter, filing her painted nails. I liked her style. I'd spent a full year as a goth; my parents hit the roof when I strolled in with raven-coloured hair, blue lipstick, and my eyebrow and nose pierced. I won't mention my attire. When they came back to earth, they sat me down and told me the phase would pass. I told them they were seeing the real me. Though a year later, I discovered another trend.

In the shop, an older couple loitered at the back. I watched as they examined ornaments and old vases; they each picked one up, looked underneath, then placed it back. Another elderly woman stared at the massive array of autobiographies.

I browsed the shoes and handbags; I had my own vast collection of bags, flats, and pumps at home, now destined to be bagged up and donated to charity. I used to add to my collection at least once a month—often my purchase would be from a charity shop.

James never approved; he hated the thought of wearing clothes and shoes that had belonged to another person—or 'a deceased person,' as he would say. But I would remind him of how much money I saved.

I think I got the habit from my grandad. When we went on walks and passed a skip, he would often end up dragging a discarded item out. 'One man's junk is another man's treasure,' he would say.

Now, I regretted my savvy buys; James would never have been able to afford all the gifts he no doubt wooed Clare with if I'd bought items brand new.

Excited voices from the back of the shop made me turn my head. The excitement faded to hushed whispers, and I edged past the woman stood in the book section to hear better.

'Yes, it is, Herbie,' whispered the woman.

'It can't be,' said Herbie as he scratched his head. 'You know Hank comes in here every day. There's no chance he missed it, Kathleen.'

'I'm telling you, Herb, it's the Royal Dalton Spanish Lady. Look at the veil and dress she's wearing!' Her voice rose as she spoke.

'Shh! Don't tell the whole shop.'

'Miss, miss!' Kathleen called to the girl behind the counter.

'Yeah,' she answered, continuing to file her nails.

'Can you tell me when this item came in?'

'Dunno.' She shrugged. 'Lunchtime, maybe?'

'See, I told you, Herb.'

'See, what? That doesn't confirm anything. Do you really

think Hank missed this?'

'I bet he hasn't seen it yet if it came in at lunch. It's only ten bob, Herb. If I'm right, it could be worth five, six hundred or more!' she exclaimed.

'Alright, Kathleen, you win…'

Their interaction made me smile. I sensed dear old Kathleen won a lot. Kathleen beamed as she handled the figure like a bomb that could go off with the slightest movement.

I crept back past the woman still stood at the books so they didn't have to walk through me. As I did, a horrendous stench filled my nostrils. No wonder she'd stayed away from others in the shop.

'Jeez, is that your backside?' Kathleen said as she walked past her.

'Whoa,' Herbie spluttered in between coughs. 'That's definitely not mine.'

The elderly woman didn't even flinch as they walked past; she had to be deaf or plain ignorant. I had to get out of there. I laughed hard as I left the shop, so much so a clothes rack started to spin. I ran as fast as I could and prayed I hadn't given one of the shoppers a heart attack.

Daniel had told me my emotions could move objects, though I hadn't expected laughter to be a trigger.

The incident made me think of my mother; she liked to remind us that if we ever needed to toot in public (I loved how she would only say *toot*) that we should stand near an older person. Her face would be deadpan serious as she described how older people don't care about their bodily functions, that they will happily let one go. James, my father, and I would let her finish, then we would roar with laughter.

The thought made me want to find a way of telling her she'd

been right; she'd been right about a lot of things. Mainly, I should have seen more of the world; shame I was only getting the chance now I'd died.

The thoughts of my mother made me think of the woman stood in the shop. She'd been stood there an awfully long time, and she hadn't moved an inch the entire time I was there. I stopped in my tracks and headed back to the shop.

Kathleen and Herbie had long gone, but the woman still stood there, and the shop assistant continued to file her nails—I wondered how she had any left.

I went over to the woman and looked at her face. Her expression was blank; she didn't do anything except blink. She had no belongings with her. No bag. Nothing.

Her arms hung down by her sides; she wore a thick silver bangle and a gold wedding band.

I looked back at the assistant. She seemed oblivious to the woman's presence.

I waved my hands in front of the woman's face. Nothing.

I glanced again at the bracelet; it didn't match the rest of her outfit. She wore slacks and a rain mac. I thought I saw writing on it, so I got down on my hands and knees to look closer at it.

Sure enough, it was a medical identity bracelet with her name, her condition, and a phone number; she had dementia. I was in no position to help, but the shop assistant could—*if only I could get her attention.*

Everything I had done until now had been random or a complete fluke. But I had to do something to help the woman; she could have been lost for hours.

I paced the short aisle. The only objects at my disposal were the books she was staring at. But these weren't little paperback books; they were thick, hardback books. If I could at least knock one onto the floor...

I stilled my mind and focused as I attempted to push one—but it wouldn't budge. I glanced at the woman; a single tear trickled down her cheek.

Oh no! Please, don't cry.

I tried again, and not one or two fell, but almost the entire shelf. Out of habit, I jumped out of the way of their fall, but several fell through me, regardless.

'Yes!' I yelled.

'What's going on over there?' the assistant said, walking over. 'What have you done?' she asked as she saw the heap of books.

Then she looked at the woman and noticed the tear streak on her face. The assistant took her hand, the same hand with the bracelet.

'Oh, sweetheart!' she said, inspecting it. 'Come with me into the back. I'll make you a nice cup of tea and call your family.'

'Thank you,' the woman whispered. 'Thank you.'

* * *

The East End beckoned me; tales of gangsters and the criminal underworld had fascinated me ever since my gran sat me on her lap and filled my head with stories of the year she spent in London at nineteen.

My father said his mother had never left our hometown, that she'd made it all up to keep me quiet or send me to sleep. But I knew my grandmother told the truth. Her eyes twinkled every time I begged her to repeat her tales over and over; I could never get enough.

Though, I could never get her to tell me why she had gone to London in the first place—she took the secret to her grave. I'd asked her sister, my great aunt, if she knew what had happened, but she refused to entertain the conversation too.

When I arrived, I headed for The Blind Beggar pub. My gran had worked in a bakery close by; she told me the pub was a regular haunt for the Kray twins and other gangster-type people. The pub had remained, despite its dark history, though it had some good history too. I'd learnt William Booth started the Salvation Army there; I think that's why Gran donated money to them.

A group of nine or ten people stood huddled together outside the pub. As I got closer, I heard a man recount the night Ronnie Kray shot George Cornell. By chance, I'd stumbled upon a tour. I listened to the tour guide until a man exited the pub, and I seized the opportunity to enter without drawing attention to my presence.

The pub had a warm, homely feel to it with its dark-oak bar, red walls, and lit fireplace. The smell of wood wax hung in the air, reminding me of my grandad. He always waxed wood, never lacquered it. He said wax was all that was needed.

I found a small round table in a corner and I sat on a stool so I could see the bar. I tried to picture the atmosphere and clientele from the swinging sixties; there would have been a lot less women here in those days, if any at all.

Three mature women stood at a table near me, sharing a bottle of Pinot noir. They wore suits and heels that would have crippled my feet in minutes if I had to wear them. They chatted about 'the good old days' when people helped each other in the community and that 'nothing had been right since Margaret Thatcher gained power.' I lost interest when they mentioned her name.

I scanned the room for another group to eavesdrop on. Out

CHAPTER SIX

the corner of my eye, I saw a large, well-built man with no hair, heading for the women. He had a purple scar on his right cheek and wore a smart suit with a white handkerchief in his top pocket.

He appeared to be either the landlord or a doorman, the way he sized everybody up. He stopped at their table, then turned and looked my way. I couldn't tell if he had seen me or not. His lip curled—*not* in a sexy, Elvis-like way—and he raised a shovel-like hand and pointed at me.

'Don't think for *one minute* you can come in here and upset my regulars,' he said in a thick, gruff voice.

I gulped and clutched my bag to my chest. I looked from the man to the door and back again. Before I had the chance to move, he loomed over me and blocked my view. If I'd been alive, my bowels would have loosened, and I'd be as white as the head on a pint of beer. He opened his mouth in such a way I thought he'd take my head off. I spoke before he could cause me any harm.

'I'm sorry, I've not been passed long. I don't know all the rules yet,' I rambled.

'What business have you here? You never visited here when you were alive; I would remember,' he said, arms folded.

'My gran told me about this place; she worked nearby when she was younger,' I said, looking back to the doors.

'What's your gran's name?' he asked.

'Elsie Johnson. It would have been Elsie Woods back then.'

'Pretty little thing… Worked in the bakery around the corner? Was that her?' he asked and unfolded his arms.

I nodded. 'Yes, she said she worked in a bakery nearby. Did you know her well?' I asked, relieved, as his demeanour had softened.

'Nah, I was just a young boy then. She was a newcomer. News travelled fast in those days when a stranger arrived. I was told she was a sweet girl, but she didn't stay long. Went back home, I think. You can't visit the bakery; it's been knocked down now. Turned into flats.' He looked away as though he was picturing it.

'Oh. Well, I'm glad to have spoken to someone who was around then. I didn't mean any disrespect by coming in. I was curious, that's all; this existence is all new to me.'

'I'll let it slide. I like to keep an eye on my regulars. It's rare to have random spirits popping in. I have to make sure they don't get up to any mischief; I won't be getting any trouble off you, will I?' he said and thrust his chest out.

'No, sir,' I said with a wry smile.

'Excellent,' he said. 'Now, I'll be leaving you; I need to keep an eye on things.'

I exhaled slowly as I watched him return to the bar and stand in the corner. He folded his arms as he scanned the room and kept a watchful eye on the clientele.

I had met yet another spirit who pertained to still have a job. It made me wonder if I had missed something—should I have gone back to my office?

A vintage clock on the wall told me I had a few hours until I had to be back at The Lion's Head, so I decided to walk around Whitechapel for a while, then take a slow stroll back. I wanted to be back in plenty of time; I hated tardiness. There's nothing worse than showing up late. I hated it when I was alive, and that hadn't gone away.

I waited for the door to open so I could slip out. As I loitered, I looked back at the former owner, and he nodded at me. Both doors opened as a group of young men entered, and I took my

CHAPTER SIX

chance to leave.

I meandered around, looking in shop windows and watching people go about their nightly routines, picking up food and walking their dogs. Somehow, I found myself walking up a low-lit cobbled alleyway straight from the Victorian era.

Dusk had fallen, and fog had descended over this part of London town. I never liked fog; it always crept out of nowhere and made hidden childhood insecurities come bubbling to the surface. I turned to go back the other way to escape, but it swirled up behind me and forced me to carry on.

With each step I took, the fog got thicker and thicker. My pace slowed, my imagination ran wild. I had nothing to fear, I told myself. I was already dead, after all.

I squinted to see better. I thought I saw a face, but I couldn't be sure. What if it was the shadowy figure that had been following me earlier? I hadn't sensed or seen whatever it was since I left the charity shop. Though that didn't mean it wasn't in front of me now.

I stopped as I heard the sound of footsteps echoing all around me. I scanned left and right, up, and down again; I couldn't see a thing. Then the footsteps faded into the distance.

I tightened the grip on my bag and tried to focus on what little of the path I could see in front of me.

As I continued, I finally saw what I must have spotted to begin with; a low hanging sign had a smiling pig face on it. I laughed. It was a comical butcher's sign.

I loosened the grip on my bag when a pair of arms emerged from the fog and a screaming face followed.

The apparition pushed me out of its way, sending me sprawling to the ground.

'Holy F-ing shit!' I yelled.

I peeped through my fingers. The fog had vanished, and I was alone in a crumpled heap on the ground, unhurt but confused.

Something touched my shoulder, and I scrambled to my feet.

A tiny older woman stood in front of me. She had a purple rinse and wore an apron that looked to be smeared with jam. At least I hoped it was jam…

'It's okay, dear, nothing to be scared of,' the woman said in a gentle voice. 'I think you are a little lost, my pet.'

I looked at her and back down the alley, bemused and wondering what the hell had happened. How could another spirit push me over, and with such force? I didn't even know we could touch each other, let alone feel it. I cursed myself for not attempting to shake Daniel's hand when we met.

'You shouldn't be walking around these streets if you don't know where you are.'

'What the hell just happened?' I asked the woman; my voice quivered.

'This happens quite frequently—as long as I can remember, anyway. She rushes past and then she is gone. She is a lost spirit—or lost soul, as some call them. All she can remember is her final thoughts, and she replays them every few nights. Lost spirits don't know how to move on,' she sighed.

'What happened to her?' I asked.

'I don't know,' she said as she retrieved a hanky from her sleeve to wipe her mouth.

'Well, who's chasing her?' It was obvious she was trying to get away from something—or someone.

'I don't know that, either. Let me show you the way back to the main road; this isn't the place for you, my dear.'

I let her take my arm to guide me. I sensed she did know

who had chased her, but for some reason was reluctant to tell me.

'Thank you... I didn't know we could touch each other.' My voice still wavered.

'Oh, are you a new spirit, my dear?'

'Yes, a little over a week,' I told her as I looked behind me, wondering if the screaming woman would return.

'Ah, I see. Well, yes, we can touch each other, just the same as you could touch someone when you were living,' she said, patting my arm. 'Hasn't anyone told you the cans and cannots yet?'

'Nope, but I'm meeting someone tonight who is hopefully going to help me.'

'Good, good. Here we are, dear,' the woman said as we walked out onto the main road. 'Do you know where you're going from here?'

'Yes, I think so. Thank you.'

'You're welcome, dear.'

'Before I go, is there no way to stop the loop? Surely something can be done to help her?' I asked.

The woman shrugged. 'I don't think so. She is oblivious to anyone and everything around her. Her sole focus is her own path.'

'That doesn't seem fair on her,' I said.

'When people pass at the hands of another, the reoccurrence happens,' said the woman.

'So, you *do* know what happened to her,' I pressed.

The woman crossed her arms and stepped back. 'I've said too much. I've got to go.'

She turned and hurried back the way we had come.

That poor soul, I thought. It didn't seem fair that she had to spend her time stuck in a loop because of the actions of another. And there was nothing I could do to help. Why are the angels letting this happen?

I shuffled on as I replayed the scene in my head. I thought my new status meant I would be safe wherever I went. I knew then I had to learn more about this life—sharpish.

With a fresh set of worries and doubts to contend with, I made my way back to The Lion's Head with trepidation in every step I took.

Chapter Seven

I made it back to the pub on time, the earlier incident still dancing in my mind, but I wasn't going to let it get in the way.

The jukebox played but was barely audible over the noise of the pub-goers. I scanned the room for Frankie G but couldn't see him. There were spirits packed into every space and seat, poised in anticipation of the night's events.

A spotlight illuminated the stage, and an empty spot appeared at the bar. I squeezed in and waited.

The song on the jukebox ended, and the crowd erupted into applause as Frankie G walked on stage. He lapped up the attention, bowing and cupping his ears as if to say 'I can't hear you! Clap louder, won't you, please?' After a minute, he signalled for the crowd to simmer down.

'Ladies and gentlemen, in just a few moments, the man you have all been waiting for will be on this stage. Make some noise for the one, the only, Henry!' He had to yell the end of his announcement over the swelling noise of the audience as the room exploded into loud applause, whistles, and yells.

'Caroline?' someone said in my ear and tapped me on the shoulder.

I hadn't noticed the woman approach me, with all the

excitement in the room. She stood next to me, around my age. She had dark, wavy hair, a pale complexion, and her red lipstick had bled into the fine lines around her mouth. Her t-shirt said, 'dirty rotten scoundrels,' which didn't fill me with confidence. Her stance and demeanour made me want to flee the pub and hide at home in a corner.

'Are you Caroline?' she said, tapping her foot.

'Yes, no, yes, I'm sorry,' I stumbled.

The woman rolled her eyes and tutted. 'Come with me.'

I hesitated to move. 'Where are we going?'

'Don't look so worried. Frankie G told me you were coming tonight. Watch the show with me and my friends, then we'll chat afterwards, okay?' She smiled, but it didn't reach her eyes. I wondered if the spirit world played havoc with all spirits' emotions or if this was just the way she was.

'Sure,' I whispered and tucked my bag in close.

I followed the woman to a round table where her friends sat. She introduced herself as Jane, then gave quick introductions for the rest of the group.

The first man she introduced as Mr Jones, no first name. He had a slim stature and wore a brown, paisley shirt. If I had to guess, he looked around twenty years old. He also had different coloured eyes, which reminded me of someone, but I couldn't quite place my finger on it.

The second man went by Benny the T, she told me. He offered no explanation, and I didn't ask. He sat with a smile plastered to his face and a cup of tea in front of him that a barmaid would replace every thirty minutes. He clearly loved tea, though he could no longer drink it.

The last of the group was Mary; she wore a knitted jumper with a cat on it and had a mass of thick, red curls.

CHAPTER SEVEN

After the pleasantries, I turned to speak to Jane, but she told me to be quiet and watch the stage.

The crowd became rowdier, and they chanted 'Henry' over and over. An invisible piano started to play, and a man walked on the stage.

'Oh. My. God!' I did a double take and almost leapt out of my seat.

Crowd members shushed me, and I sank back into my chair. 'Isn't that—'

But Jane told me to button it before I could finish my sentence.

'But he—' I attempted again.

'Yes, we know. No one talks about his past, *okay?*' she said through clenched teeth.

I watched, mouth agape, as a former king grabbed the mic and started to rap. The pub went wild.

I glanced around to see if the others had the same view as me, but they all loved it. I wanted to yell out 'Are you kidding me?' but I heeded Jane's warning and in the end thought, 'What the hell,' and joined in.

When Henry disappeared in the blink of an eye and the mic fell to the floor, a mixture of boos and hisses erupted from the horde of people.

'Where did he go?' I asked Jane.

She titled her head. 'Okay, you have a lot to learn, don't you?'

'I guess so,' I shrugged. 'I've got a lot of questions to ask.'

Jane looked me over, then whipped her hair back. 'Okay, who thinks Caroline should tell us a bit about herself?' she asked the table.

A couple nodded their heads.

'Great, okay. So, Caroline, fill us in, okay?' said Jane.

I shuffled in my chair as the group waited for me to speak. 'Well, I died just over a week ago. Car accident,' I told them.

'Awful way to go that, hen,' said Mary in a Scottish accent.

'I guess...' I said.

I hadn't thought about it much. I couldn't really remember the accident, and there were worse ways to go, I figured. As I tried to remember the crash, the words of the police officer echoed in my mind about James not braking. I wondered if I should try to find out more.

'Hey.' Jane clicked her fingers in front of my face.

'Oh, sorry, yes,' I said and gave my head a shake. 'I spent the first week with my parents; I wanted to make sure they'd be okay. Then I went to the beach and met a guy called Daniel. He told me—'

'Beach Daniel?' interrupted Mary, her eyes fixed on Jane.

'Yes,' I said. The table rattled and almost levitated off the ground. 'He... saved me from going on the... the beach...' I continued, my eyes focused on a name scratched into the table which wobbled in front of me. *What's going on?*

'Easy now, hen,' Mary said to Jane.

The table stilled, and Jane tapped on the wood, then nodded at Mary. I didn't speak. I watched and waited for the long silence to be broken.

'He... We... Look, we used to date, okay?' said Jane.

'When you were alive?' I asked, trying to sound nonchalant. I didn't care, but I wanted to know why Jane cared so much.

'No, I met him after I died, okay? Right here, actually. You do know we can touch each other, don't you?' said Jane as she glanced at Mary. Then Mary winked at Benny the T.

I nodded and told the group about the unfortunate incident with the lost soul. I tried to sound as though I knew what a lost soul was, but I really didn't have a clue. Jane's reaction at the sound of Daniel's name still intrigued me, though, and I pushed to find out a little bit more about him.

'So, Daniel used to come here?' I said, my finger tracing the name etched on the table, though I couldn't feel the carving. The group glanced at each other, but no one spoke. 'I thought his job was to protect newbies on the beach,' I added.

The group started to laugh—even Benny the T, who hadn't said a word all night.

'Pfft, that's not his job, hen,' chuckled Mary.

'Us spirits don't have jobs, okay. Though how we choose to spend our time differs from one spirit to the next. Some go back to their old lives and follow their previous routines—going to work, home, *et cetera*. Others can't process what's happened. They get lost and replay their dying moments like the woman you saw in the alley. There are no hard and fast rules here,' said Jane.

'Right, I see. I think I'm beginning to understand things a little better,' I said.

'How long did you get, hen? If you don't mind me asking,' asked Mary.

'Ten years.'

The group whistled.

'Okay, I'm guessing you aren't going back to your old life or your old job?' Jane paused, then tapped on the table. 'I mean, you wouldn't be here if you were,' she said and tossed her hair again.

'I'm not as it goes,' I offered. I didn't want to give them anything else. The atmosphere around Jane and her little group didn't sit well with me. There'd been a lot of sideways glances and little taps and knocks on the table, as if they were having their own private conversation without me.

'What will you be doing, then? Not chasing after my leftovers, I hope?' Jane smirked.

'Now, hen, what have we talked about?' Mary said to Jane before I could defend myself.

'She *has* asked a lot of questions about him,' Jane retorted.

'I want to learn how to scare someone,' I interjected before they could continue to talk about me as if I had left the room. The group stared at me. I shifted to sit bolt upright in my chair. 'Is that possible?' I asked them.

'Yes, it's possible, hen. Some spirits have been known to give a scare or two,' said Mary as she looked at Jane. 'You have to be careful, though. The thrill can overwhelm some spirits. Isn't that right, Jane?'

'Hmm, okay. Yes, what she said,' Jane uttered, though she appeared to be far away from the conversation now.

'Well, what can I do? How can I scare someone?' I asked eagerly. I wanted to do more than knock a few books off a shelf.

'We won't know that; you'll just have to see what works for you. But we can tell you our favourites, okay,' said Jane, back from wherever her mind had drifted off to. 'But you must be careful. Daniel once scared someone so badly they fell down some stairs and had a heart attack.'

'Oh my god!' I'd only met Daniel briefly, but I never thought he'd be capable of that. Perhaps that's why he spends his time saving souls at the beach; to atone for his sins.

'He doesn't seem so nice now, does he, Caroline?' said Jane, her voice laced with sarcasm, which I chose to ignore.

I shook my head. 'I guess not.'

Hearing what Daniel had done made me a little wary of

CHAPTER SEVEN

seeking further information so I could scare Clare. I didn't want to hurt her. So I reasoned with myself; I could listen to what they had to say and decide for myself if I should continue.

'Do you still want to know our favourites?' asked Mary.

'Sure,' I said.

'Okay,' said Jane. 'Mine are putting thoughts into people's minds by placing a hand over their head. Making someone change direction by tapping them on the shoulder. But those are powerful actions for the most experienced of spirits—not for beginners like yourself.' She gave me a quick sideways glance, then continued. 'You oughta try crouching down on floorboards to make them creak. Your turn, Mary, you've been around longer than me.'

'Och, it's been a while for me,' she said, turning a lose curl around her finger. 'You've got to be careful in houses these days. Damn PVC; worst thing to be invented if you're a spirit. Now homes are all sealed up, so we must stick to the corners.' She shook her head.

'Yes, Michael did mention that,' I agreed, though I hated the thought of being stuck in a corner for ten years.

'He's right,' Mary continued. 'Homes used to have a lot more drafts. It wouldn't matter where you went. Homes are far too warm for us now, and there's less room to hide. I try to avoid them when possible. If I do have to go in, I force all the dirt from the radiators into one so the heating stops working.' Mary laughed, her hair bouncing as she did.

'Anything else?' I asked, frowning. I wanted something else; I didn't like the sound of that.

'Usual stuff. Moving objects from one place to another or hiding them.' Mary waved her hands back and forth. 'Making lights flicker. Banging on pipes is an oldie but a goodie,' she added.

'That's helpful—*really*. Thank you. But how do I do all these things? I mean, I've done the odd thing…' I offered.

The group eyed each other, seemingly deciding between them who was going to answer the question.

I shuffled nervously in my seat.

Come on, I've got ten years not a hundred.

'It takes patience and practice,' Mary eventually answered with a sigh. 'If you have enough determination and you really want to do it, you can do anything.'

I resisted rolling my eyes. The words weren't enough; I needed them to show me. That seemed to have been how it had worked in the charity shop, but I wanted to learn some consistency so it would work every time.

'Okay, anything else?' asked Jane.

'Yes, two things. What happened to Henry? And what else goes on here? Do you just get together and chat?'

'You take the first one, Mary.'

'Oh, that happens to him all the time, hen. He's a popular man,' said Mary.

I cocked my head. 'I'm sorry, I don't understand. What happens all the time?'

'When a person of the living persuasion has strong thoughts about a person that has passed over, it can pull their spirit to them.' Mary looked over her shoulder, then whispered, 'Hasn't it happened to you yet, hen?'

'Ooh…' I said, recalling the moment I'd been pulled from the park to the morgue. 'Is that what that was?'

Why would anyone want to think of him? I wondered. Then I thought about my parents. I hadn't been pulled back to them yet, which could only be a good thing.

CHAPTER SEVEN

'I'm glad, pet,' she said and patted my arm. 'I would hate to think you'd been forgot about—and in such a short time. Let me tell you, it happens more frequently as your loved ones move out of the denial stage.'

I frowned. 'No, I don't think I'll be forgotten yet. Can I ask another thing? Will I ever get used to the sensation I get when I move from place to place? It's like being pulled inside out!'

They all laughed and nodded.

'Okay, to answer your other question, we have acts on stage, speed dating, all sorts. There's always something going on,' said Jane.

'Speed dating… I think I'd like to give that a try,' I said.

'Are you not married?' Jane said and reached out for my left hand.

I pulled my hand into my lap, out of her grasp.

'Technically I am, but I won't be seeing him anytime soon,' I muttered darkly.

'The plot thickens.' Jane snorted. 'Okay, well, speed dating is the last Friday of every month.'

'You should go mingle now, hen.' Mary smiled. 'Not much else happening tonight. And just a warning for you, pet, the spiritual plane isn't as black and white as you may think. There are a lot of grey areas.'

I nodded and got up from the table. I knew when I was no longer welcome.

'And Caroline? Stay away from Daniel, okay?' Jane said, and her eyes flashed, which I didn't think was possible.

Wow, talk about jealousy.

I hurried from the table and found an empty one to sit at. I needed time to process the night's events. I didn't want to give Jane the impression she'd rattled me, so I sat confidently as I scanned the room.

I watched as spirits left. Most disappeared, others went the traditional way. I figured those that lingered had to be regulars. I hadn't frequented pubs that often before my death, but I felt The Lion's Head had to be like others. The jukebox played, spirits sat and laughed and joked, and some played cards and dominos. I wondered if the current owners knew what went on after hours. Had they gone into the bar late one night and seen cards being dealt by invisible hands or dominos being shuffled, causing them to run away with fright?

A strange figure caught my eye. The only way I could describe him was a mixture of Obi-Wan Kenobi and Friar Tuck. He walked with his hands clasped in front of him, as though he would start to pray any minute. He wasn't particularly tall or large, though his stomach did protrude. If it weren't for his outfit, I don't think I would have given him a second glance.

He made a beeline for Jane's table. His arrival had not gone unnoticed, as conversations died down to faint murmurs. Jane clocked him first. She tapped on the table, and the group sat upright in their chairs and watched the man approach.

The man had piqued my interest now. I didn't know the group well, but I could sense the worry and tension in the air.

I thought perhaps he came from wherever Michael, Az, and Raff dwelled, though that thought dwindled after he shared a few words with the group, then headed in my direction.

This is not good, not good at all.

He reached my table, hands still clasped in front of him.

'Hello,' he said in an unexpected dulcet tone.

'Hello,' I replied.

'May I sit?' he asked.

'Go ahead,' I said, though wary of all the eyes focused on me.

CHAPTER SEVEN

'I'm Eisen,' said the strangely dressed man.

'Caroline,' I said. My eyes drifted to Jane's table. Jane made no attempt to disguise the fact she was staring at me.

'Yes, I know. News travels fast,' said Eisen.

'Great, there's also a spirit grapevine,' I said folding my arms. 'Am I in trouble or something?'

Eisen cocked his head. 'No, not at all. Why would you think that? Have you done something you shouldn't have?' he said, looking at Jane's table.

'Oh, I don't know...' My voice was thick with cynicism. 'Maybe because everyone is looking at me, and I don't know who you are.'

He quickly glanced at Jane again, who turned back to her friends. 'No, you aren't in trouble. Not yet, anyway.'

My eyebrows furrowed at his comment. 'Well, I'm leaving now. Was there something you wanted?'

Eisen smiled but said nothing. He watched me, though he appeared to be engaged in thought. I didn't want to stay any longer. Conversations had resumed, yet I could still feel the odd pair of eyes on me.

'If I can't help you with anything, I'll be off,' I said and got up to leave.

'Sit down, please,' Eisen finally spoke.

He had an authoritative tone to his voice that made me obey his request.

'Caroline, you really should be careful who you make friends with.' Eisen glared at Jane again.

I relaxed a little. He seemed to want to watch out for me.

'Oh, I will. I just needed a little help from them, that's all,' I said, fiddling with my bag.

Eisen frowned, then nodded. I wondered what he knew

about Jane that I didn't.

I studied his outfit a bit closer. He wore a robe made of a thick hessian-like material, and a rope wrapped around his waist had been tied off in fancy knots. Around his neck hung a ring of twisted metal that opened at his throat.

'Why are you dressed like that?' I blurted. 'I mean, have you been to a comic-book convention or something? I'm half expecting two droids to come along any moment.' I coughed down a giggle.

'Huh? Comic—what?' Eisen said, clearly taken back by my apparent insult. 'This is what I've always worn,' he told me, unclasping his hands to straighten the robes out.

I tried to hide my pained expression behind my hair. 'I'm sorry, it was only a joke.'

Eisen clutched his round belly and laughed.

'What's so funny?'

'Just the look on your face.' He continued to laugh. 'I'm what you might know as a Pagan, though we've had many names, and I've heard every joke and jibe there is going.' He rolled his eyes.

'Are you a spirit like me?' I asked, my mouth slowly tugging upwards.

'Technically, yes, but I have more freedom and gifts than most. I can travel to any time and place and can also pass through to any realm.'

'Yeah, right,' I said, then clasped a hand over my mouth. I hadn't meant to say it out loud.

'A non-believer, I see,' he said and stroked his chin. 'Come on, take my hand,' he said, reaching over.

I tucked my hands underneath me. 'I'm not going anywhere with you. How do I know you aren't the Lord of Darkness come to take me away?'

'Pfft,' he spluttered, sweeping the air with his hand as though to wave my words away. 'Don't believe that nonsense, it's just idle tittle-tattle. You've had your time allocated, and here you will stay unless you do something incomprehensible.' His gaze turned to Jane again.

Why does he keep looking at her?

'So, I'm here for ten years… and no one can take me away?' I enquired.

'No. Now, come on, take my hand. What's the worst that could happen? You're a spirit now.'

He made a good point; I had nothing to argue with.

'Fine, I'll go,' I said, moving my handbag securely to my shoulder. 'Is it scary where we're going?'

'Scary? No,' he chuckled.

'I guess it doesn't matter, anyway. I've had these pants on for a week. I dare say you've had yours on longer. If you're wearing any at all, that is.' I laughed.

Eisen raised an eyebrow, then grabbed my hand.

Before I could blink, Eisen had moved us into a forest, and it was no longer the middle of the night. I let go of his hand and looked around.

The forest was awash with leaves that had turned a coppery gold, and spiderwebs were outlined in dew. In a small clearing, two men sat chatting with a half-built shelter nearby.

'Where are we? No…' I eyed the men's clothes; they wore ill-fitting tunics of a similar reddish-brown colour and calf-length leather boots. 'What year is this?'

'We are in the south of England, and it is 1307.'

'What! Are you crazy?' I dashed to hide behind him. 'People can't see me dressed like this; they'll think I'm a witch. I'll be burned at the stake!' I exclaimed.

He tutted. 'Witch hunts started later. No one can see you. Calm down.'

I stepped out from behind the man. 'That's fine for me, but what about you? Are you safe here? Have you got a lightsaber hidden for protection?'

Eisen rolled his eyes again. 'Ha-ha, like I've never heard that one before.'

I tilted my head at him. 'Eisen, forgive my rudeness, but you don't talk as though you're from another era.'

'You're right. I have adapted with each decade that passes. I have learnt the lingo to get down with the kids, as they say.' He did a little jig.

'Okay…' I smirked. 'But don't ever say that last part again—or dance.'

He laughed. 'I won't.'

'So, why did you bring me to this place and time?'

'See those men over there?' He pointed, and I followed his finger. 'The younger of the two is Max—I'm his spirit guide,' he said proudly.

I looked over at the man he called Max; he wasn't much younger than his companion, but he carried himself differently, almost regally, whereas the other man's shoulders were slumped. He had blue-grey eyes and a stubbly chin.

'What does that mean?' I asked.

'Max is from a special family. I've been a guide to his ancestors for many years.' Eisen pulled out a scroll and unrolled it. 'See how big his family tree is?'

I peered at the old parchment; it was at least twice my height. 'Wow…'

'Max has a unique destiny,' Eisen continued. 'I waited a long

CHAPTER SEVEN

time for him to be born. I check on him to ensure he stays on the right path. Do you understand?'

'I'm not sure,' I frowned. 'Why do you need to keep checking on him? This time has been and gone. Surely, he's fulfilled his destiny,' I remarked.

'This time still exists, and there are others like me from the spiritual realm. Their motives are different to mine. They can alter events, sometimes inadvertently or on purpose.' He looked up to the heavens, then continued: 'My loyalty is to Max. If the timeline does shift, I have to nudge him back on track, or it could be catastrophic for him.'

I raised my eyebrows. 'That sounds like some quantum physics shit I just don't understand.'

And what does it have to do with me?

'You don't need to comprehend how time exists, but I want you to understand how important it is to follow the right path. Can you take that onboard, at least?'

'Yes, I get that part.' I waved my hand. 'But I still don't understand why you brought me here. You could have just told me.'

Laughter from the two men drew my attention away. Even a nearby horse seemed to join in with their fun.

'You have a path and a unique destiny too, Caroline.'

I turned back to Eisen slowly and squinted up at him, one eyebrow raised. 'I don't think I do. *An agenda, maybe...*' I muttered that last part, thinking of Clare. 'I think perhaps the angels should have picked someone else to come back.'

Eisen hummed lightly. 'You'll see.'

I shook my head.

'Anyway, there is another reason I'm keeping a close eye on him. Max's spirit has been getting stronger for the past century…' Eisen paused to look at him. 'He has been latching on to people in your time; he replays his near-death experiences for them.'

'What does that—'

'Wait, let me finish. There is one man who has experienced Max's past life coming through into his own life, and he's even felt Max's death twice, causing him to feel his pain. It's had a profound effect on him. I do believe he might be related to Max, though I've not come across his lineage before,' Eisen said inspecting the parchment.

'All right, you've lost me now…' I said, sitting on a nearby log.

'It might mean nothing at all, or it could mean something is changing. Do you feel anything is different?'

'How on earth would I know!' I exclaimed, my hands flying either side of my head. 'I've only been this way for little over a week. I'm still figuring out my place here.'

'You're right. I just thought… No, never mind,' he said, rolling the parchment back up.

'You thought what?'

'Nothing, never mind,' he said and sat next to me.

Neither of us spoke for several moments.

'You know, it's funny you brought me to this time. My grandmother told me we are descended from royal blood that married into a Belgian family around this time. I don't know if it's true or not. She told me a lot of things…' I trailed off.

'I'm glad you brought that up. I was wondering if you knew your lineage. I never bring it up in case the person is unaware.'

'Really? She was right?' I asked.

'Of course. In fact, Max's path crossed with the Duchess, your ancestor.'

'A duchess? So, I'm connected to Max in some sort of six degrees of Kevin Bacon way?'

'Kevin… Bacon?'

I shook my head and waved my hand. 'It's just a game—you link yourself to someone in six acquaintances or less.'

He laughed. 'Well, it takes a lot more than six to connect you to Max, but yes, there is a connection of sorts.'

'Wow…' I murmured, my attention back on the man. 'So, can I talk to his spirit and ask about my family?'

Eisen shook his head. 'I'm afraid not. You aren't in the same realm as him. Plus, I always seem to be one step behind his spirit when he chooses to visit,' he sighed.

Different realms? I was overwhelmed now. I'd had a lot of information to process in the past week; more than I'd ever been given in my twenty-five years of living.

'Hang on a minute,' I said as I recalled what he'd said earlier. 'You said no one can see me, right? Does that mean you look like you've been talking to yourself for the past ten minutes?'

'Indeed, it does. However, that's a good thing. It means people stay away from me, and I can get on with my business.'

'Fair enough… Are there any other revelations you wish to share?' I asked.

'No, not particularly. Mainly, I wanted to get you out of that pub for a little while, and I also had to check on Max. I thought I may as well do both at the same time. The fact you are connected to Max is neither here nor there, for now.'

'What do you mean "for now"?'

'Nothing… Forget I said anything.'

I frowned. 'You keep saying that.'

'Hmm, I do, don't I?' He looked at Max again.

'Okay…' I sighed, long and slow. 'So… can we go back now?'

Eisen stepped in front of me. 'In a moment. I want to give you some advice first.'

'Sure. What?'

'Be careful who you make friends with—especially in that pub—or you could find yourself in a position you don't want to be in. The time you were allocated can be rescinded at any time. Don't be getting yourself into any trouble.'

'What?' I protested. 'I was never told that, and you said no one could take me away!'

'They can't as long as you stick to the rules, Caroline.'

I looked towards the sky as it started to rain lightly. Those angels had a lot to answer for when I got back up there.

'You were told the rules, weren't you?' Eisen asked. No doubt he'd seen the look of anguish on my face.

I shook my head.

'Those angels… always cutting corners these days,' he groaned, then turned to me, his expression kind but serious. 'Please, follow my advice, Caroline. Stick to the right path, find someone good to spend your time with, and maybe have a little fun along the way. Being given this time here is a privilege, not a punishment. Do something useful with it.'

'Easy for you to say,' I sighed. 'You know all the rules. I was going to try speed dating in the pub.'

'By all means still go to that pub, just find a different group of friends,' Eisen said as he patted my shoulder.

'Thank you, Eisen.'

'I've enjoyed our little trip, Caroline, so I'm going to tell you a secret. You've already met the spirit you should be spending your time with.'

'Have I? Who is it?'

'That's not for me to say. It's time we were getting back, and

CHAPTER SEVEN

you can have a think about what I've said.'

Chapter Eight

When I arrived back in the pub, Eisen had disappeared. And before anyone could approach me, I closed my eyes and thought of home.

I made it on my first attempt—no random stopovers this time around—landing in the middle of the living room. The ticking clock on the mantel was now out of sync with no-one around to wind it up.

I'd enjoyed the time I'd spent with Eisen. He had given me hope everything would be alright during my time here. I'd deal with Clare, then find my path.

But every spirit I had spoken with so far appeared to be hiding some deep, dark secret with all the vagueness I'd witnessed.

There was a lot I'd have to work out for myself.

The light patter of rain on the window filled the heavy silence, and I had the distinct impression somebody had been here.

I turned around slowly and noted the aroma of freshly brewed coffee wafting in from the kitchen. As I stepped in, I realised someone had washed and put away all the crockery and utensils that had still been out from my last day here.

I slowly crept upstairs. Our bedroom door was ajar, and a

CHAPTER EIGHT

light lit up the room. I prodded the door open.

James's top drawer was open, revealing its emptiness, and when I crossed to the wardrobe, I saw his travel case was gone too.

I sat on the bed. Of course, he would need something to wear and toiletries while he was in hospital.

Hopefully, it had been his mother who had called by, not Clare. I couldn't envisage Clare washing up with her nails or coming round this early.

I got up and checked the bathroom. On the counter sat a tear and mascara-stained tissue.

Behind me, the bedside lamp flickered, then the bulb popped, plunging everything into darkness.

I ground my teeth as I stalked from the bathroom. The trip to the pub had forced me into a state of limbo. Though Jane and her friends had told me what they could do in their forms, they hadn't really helped me discover what I could do. And I couldn't decide whether to wing it and show up at Clare's or wait a bit longer.

Plus, Eisen had given me other pieces of information to consider. He had told me I should spend my time with someone I had already met, and I trusted he knew details of my spiritual path, even if I didn't quite understand what that all meant.

I hadn't met many men so far (I presumed he meant a male figure). I made a list of my potential companions from the people I had met: the hospital porter (though I hadn't spoken to him), then I met Daniel, though I couldn't see him leaving the beach anytime soon. The landlord of The Blind Beggar pub made me feel like a naughty schoolgirl. So that left me with the spirits in The Lion's Head: Frankie G, Benny The T, Mr Jones, or 'Great Gatsby' Jack. I couldn't see myself spending time with any on the list, but I had to be open to all possibilities and take chances.

I made up my mind that I would return to the pub for speed dating on Friday. Eisen had warned me away from Jane, and I knew it would be hard to ignore her if I did return, but I saw no way of progressing without the help of the spirits there.

Speed dating wasn't for a few days, though, so I needed to find things to fill my time until I was ready to see Clare.

I walked back to the living room. Something still felt out of place. You know that feeling when you walk into your house and know someone else has been in who doesn't live there. I had it often when I lived on my own; it would usually have been my parents popping by to leave me something.

I glanced at the mantle again; a photo faced down. I knew the photo well without having to look. The wooden frame contained a picture of our first dance. We seemed happy in that moment, and I remembered it like yesterday; everyone in the room had melted away as I looked into James's eyes.

The day will forever be tainted now with Clare's betrayal and her scheme to steal James away from me.

Without thinking, I reached for the photo and slung it across the room. It hit the wall with a crack, then dropped to the floor. It felt good to have released my anger and frustration on something.

I reached for another frame, this one held a picture of us just after James proposed, but my fingers couldn't grasp it.

'Huh.'

I tried again, but it wouldn't budge. Everything I tried to do was always hit and miss.

I flopped onto the sofa with a huff, not even sinking into

the cushions as I'd used to. It was around seven o'clock in the morning. I knew from the sound of my neighbour's car; he left later for work on a Tuesday. Time was funny in the spiritual plane. It seemed to speed up and slow down whenever it wanted to.

I didn't want to cause myself any undue stress by worrying about what I could and couldn't do—I'd only been like this for just over a week, and I had plenty of time to educate myself.

I considered going to see some friends, but I couldn't risk it yet. If I got upset at the sight of seeing them, it might trigger my emotions, and I didn't want to draw attention to myself and freak them out.

Instead, I followed my normal routine in the hope I'd pick up some skills along the way. An easy task, since I didn't work Tuesdays.

I started with some yoga, carrying out all the poses with ease, my muscles and limbs no longer fighting the positions I forced them into. Next on the list would be laundry, then a long soak in the bath. Those tasks were pointless now, and following my routine was suddenly pointless too.

I was at a loss. Other spirits seemed to have a purpose. I only wanted to get revenge, but I didn't have the know-how to do that.

I paced the living room floor, then quickly headed for the kitchen, slamming the door behind me as I entered. I couldn't escape it, the memories of my time here poured out. Everywhere I looked I was reminded of James and the life we'd built together. I had to get out of the house.

I walked out of the front door and slammed it shut. I didn't care if anyone saw, though the early hour did provide some cover.

The street I lived on was lined with cherry blossom trees. They were in full bloom, reminding me of candy floss and visits to the fair as a child.

As I walked, I was sure I could feel someone watching me. I scanned the vicinity and saw nothing. There was hardly a soul about as I made it to the high street.

I looked behind me, certain someone was there.

A figure stepped out from a shop doorway.

'Hello again, Caroline,' said Daniel.

I gasped and stopped. 'Get away from me,' I said, heeding Jane's warning.

He ignored me and stepped closer. 'I need to speak with you.'

'Don't come any closer. I know what you did!' I spat. 'Now, leave me alone.'

I turned and ran as fast as I could, snubbing his shouts and pleads for me to stop.

The nearer I got to the square in the town centre, the louder I heard a person whistling. And the more I listened in to identify the tune and ignore Daniel, the more I felt compelled to follow the sound.

'Don't follow the whistling!' Daniel yelled behind me.

I continued to disregard his calls as he followed and turned on to a side street to track the source.

The tune got louder, and I saw a crowd of people following a council litter-picker. As I approached, I guessed they had to be spirits. When he took a step, so did the crowd, though it wasn't obvious why.

I checked behind me. Daniel hadn't followed me onto the narrow street.

'Shut up, will ya!' one of the crowd members shouted.

CHAPTER EIGHT

I shuffled my way into the crowd and whispered, 'What's going on?' thinking I was about to witness an amazing spectacle.

'Damn whistling again, that's what. Third time this week I've been caught out,' an angry man responded.

'I'm sorry, I don't understand.' I looked around, hoping someone would fill in the blanks.

'When people whistle, it draws us in,' said a man with a kind voice.

'What?' I scoffed. 'So, we just follow him till he stops?'

'Yep, afraid so,' a woman to my right piped in.

'I'm not having that. I've got better things to do,' I told the group. I tried to walk in the opposite direction but only got a few paces before an invisible barrier bounced me back into the fold.

'What the hell!' I yelled and brushed myself down.

'Told you so,' the same female voice retorted.

I fell in with the rest of the group. The man showed no signs of stopping anytime soon. He seemed to enjoy his job as he whistled his merry tunes. The group must have grown to thirty spirits along the way as he weaved up and down the side streets.

No one spoke, and I quickly grew bored of pacing the chewing-gum laced pavements. How this man couldn't sense our presence was beyond my comprehension.

I decided to come up with a nickname for him when there was a jostle behind me, and someone pushed in on my left. I felt no curiosity to check out my new companion as my shoulders hunched up closer to my ears.

'This is ridiculous,' said the man next to me.

'Hmm,' I muttered, not in the mood to engage in conversation with a stranger.

A couple who were holding hands in front of me disappeared.

'Hey, no fair! How come they get to leave?' I whined.

'Probably needed by a friend or a family member,' the man at my side answered. 'It's nice to see you again, Caroline.'

I jerked my head up as I realised who my companion was. 'Eisen! What are you doing here?'

'Oh, just came to say hello,' he smirked.

'Fine. Hello,' I snapped.

Eisen started laughing and clutched his stomach. He continued to laugh even as he side-stepped a cyclist in a flashy suit with his trousers tucked in his socks. I would have grinned at the sight, but I couldn't seem to turn my scowl around.

I folded my arms. 'What's so funny?'

He snorted. 'Just watching you lot following this man.' He pointed at the bald patch on the back of the whistler's head. 'It's hilarious.'

'Well, you're stuck here too. That's not so funny,' I said and tossed my hair back.

'I'm not trapped here. I can leave anytime I want,' he said.

'Well, *hoorah* for you. Now you've said hello, you can leave,' I said, my shoulders hunching again.

'Now, now, no need to be rude, Caroline,' he said, wagging his finger.

I groaned, hanging my head to stare at the pavement, wishing it would open up and swallow me whole. 'Sorry…'

'Caroline, do you think you're on the right path yet?'

'What do you mean?'

'I told you to find the right path. Do you think this,' he motioned with his hands, 'is it?'

CHAPTER EIGHT

'I doubt it.' I shrugged. 'Plus, it's only been a couple of hours since I saw you.'

I looked at the spirits around me and frowned. What about them? Did they have their own paths or destinies? Why was Eisen so interested in me? What made me so special?

'It's not been hours on my plane. Come on, Caroline. I thought you were smarter than that. Didn't you listen to anything I said?'

'I did... but everything you say is cryptic. If you know what I should be doing, why don't you just tell me?' I sniped.

'Well, that would be too easy, wouldn't it?' he said, side stepping a woman dragging a shopping trolley behind her.

I sighed. I didn't know what Eisen expected from me. I wasn't psychic, and I didn't care for his games. And why didn't he let the living pass through him?

'If you aren't going to tell me, can you at least get this guy to stop whistling?' I asked.

'I could, but I'm not going to. He's in a good mood, and I'm not about to wreck that. Who knows what the consequences would be.'

'Fine,' I muttered.

'Two things before I go: one, go and see your friend Tamara. And two, I've been cloaked to the rest of these spirits. You've been talking to yourself for the past five minutes.'

Eisen disappeared, his chortling laugh echoing for a few seconds after his departure. I looked around to see a few spirits had shifted away from me.

Great, just great.

The group carried on. We had that many cheesed off spirits that we started to look like extras from a zombie movie. We'd nearly reached the bottom of the high street when our group leader, whom I'd nicknamed Dave, stopped to talk to a homeless man sat in a doorway. The group dispersed as quickly as they could. Some ran off, and others vanished before Dave could resume.

I considered Eisen's visit. If he knew of my destiny, why wouldn't he just tell me? Surely it would make it easier on everyone. And what the heck had Daniel wanted? He was a long way from his 'job.'

* * *

I wanted to be defiant against Eisen's request and not do as he'd asked. After all, he wouldn't share anything with me. But by the evening, curiosity had won me over, and I thought of Tamara, landing in her little girl's bedroom.

'Yes!' I yelled and punched the air.

A figure stirred on the bed, and I clasped my hands over my mouth, then gave my head a shake for thinking I'd woken her up. Tamara's daughter, Eliza, was four going on fourteen, so Tamara told me.

Everywhere I looked I saw a unicorn or a rainbow, and I could smell the baby shampoo Tamara used on Eliza's delicate blonde curls.

I tiptoed over to the bed and peeped at her face; a pair of blue eyes blinked up at me.

'Oh, crap.' I stumbled back into a chair filled with dozens of teddy bears. Luckily, my surprise wasn't enough to send any of them flying.

'Aunty Caz!' Eliza threw back her sheets and jumped out of bed.

'Shh!' I said, putting my finger to my lips. 'You can see me?'

CHAPTER EIGHT

'Yes, silly. Can you read me a story?'

I slumped to the floor; I'd had no idea Eliza had a gift. Tamara had never mentioned it. Perhaps she didn't know.

Eliza shifted on the spot and continued to stare at me, her expression innocent, so I composed myself and agreed to read her a story. I couldn't disappoint that little face.

'Pick a book and hop back into bed, sweet pea, and I'll read it to you,' I said.

'Yay!' She twirled round and picked her favourite book about how Santa's dogs saved Christmas. I'd read it that many times, I almost knew it by heart.

'Aunty Caz,' she said as she climbed back into bed, 'Mummy's been very sad. She said you've gone to sleep with the angels in the clouds.' She fiddled with the sheets in her chubby little hands.

'That's right, sweet pea, but the angels said I could come back and see my favourite little person. Do you know who that is?'

'Me!' She clapped her hands.

'You know it, sweet pea. Now, let's read this book, and you can go back to sleep.'

'Okay, Aunty Caz.'

Pushing the books in the charity shop had been hard, but holding the book so Eliza could see was much easier. It seemed anger and laughter weren't the only emotions that gave me strength: love was just as powerful.

By the end of page three, Eliza had fallen asleep. I placed the book back on the shelf and crept out of the room.

I leant back on the door and wanted to cry. But nothing would come. Not one tear or a sob.

I hoped I'd done the right thing staying with Eliza rather

than vanishing in front of her. I'd never forgive myself if I caused her any trauma at such a young age.

I crept downstairs in search of my friend and studied the pictures lining the wall. In one, Tamara had me on her back; we were dressed as cheerleaders for my hen night. On another, I was holding Eliza on the day she was born. It had been magical holding her in my arms. I sighed, remembering it like it was yesterday.

I located Tamara in the kitchen, drinking freshly brewed coffee; the smell permeated the entire downstairs of the house.

She made me laugh. No matter how much coffee she drank or the time of day, she could always fall asleep in the time it took to click your fingers.

I yearned to be sat with her now, drinking my own cup. It was the first time I'd truly craved a drink or food since I'd passed over.

Tamara was sat at the breakfast bar, staring at her phone. I watched as she went straight to my social media profile and sighed. I moved closer and placed a hand on her shoulder, then whispered in her ear: 'I'm okay, Tamara. Don't worry about me.' I kissed her on the cheek, then left.

Chapter Nine

There was a pen on the side that I wanted to move. The first couple of times, I couldn't even pick it up. Then, as I focused my mind on Clare, on the pain and hurt she'd caused me, all the times I should have questioned why she was so interested in James's schedule, when he would be popping by, but most of all, what an idiot I'd been for not seeing it, I could carry it a few paces before it fell to the ground.

Next, I tried the TV remote. I picked it up, switched the TV on and then took it to the other side of the room and placed it in a plant pot. James would have fun figuring that one out.

Since returning from Tamara's, I'd been practising what I could do to scare Clare. I didn't know what room she would be in or what she would be doing when I turned up, so I made it my mission to be able to do anything whatever room she was in.

I moved to the kitchen. I'd seen a film where a woman walked into her kitchen and all the cupboard doors and drawers were open; I wanted to try it.

I grabbed the handles and pulled. I mastered it quickly and danced around the kitchen as I pulled drawers open and kicked doors shut. Though I knew it wouldn't be enough to scare off Clare. I had to do more, but how?

At that point, I was drained, so I sat on the sofa to recover before trying another room. I watched the TV for a while before I headed to the bathroom to attempt turning on the taps.

As I climbed the stairs, a familiar lurching turned my stomach, and the staircase beneath me vanished unexpectedly. I fell for a few moments before landing lightly next to a bed. But it wasn't my parents' bed or Clare's. It wasn't even James's hospital bed. This one was a small double with dark purple sheets. Next to a pillow sat a worse-for-wear pink bear. It looked familiar. In fact, I was sure I'd bought it for a girl I used to babysit.

I found the owner of the bear sat in front of the mirror at her dressing table. The table was full of black make-up, and an e-reader sat open, the screen still alight.

Wow, someone is going through a goth phase.

I didn't recognise the girl at first. All I saw was a young, ashen face in the mirror, looking at her reflection as black tears rolled down her cheeks. The mirror was surrounded by photos of all shapes and sizes, though her eyes seemed to be focused on one.

I looked closer at the photo and saw a younger version of me with my arms around a young girl—a tiny copy of the girl in the mirror, though she was a shadow of her former self.

I'd been right: it was Leanne. She's sixteen, by the looks of things, almost seventeen. It's a hard age from what I remembered. Even harder now with the influx of social media platforms.

I couldn't be sure why I'd been pulled there. I hadn't seen her for years, and we hadn't kept in touch.

'Caroline, I miss you,' she said to the photo.

CHAPTER NINE

'Oh, Leanne, sweetheart. I'm here. What's wrong?' I crossed the room in a flash and knelt by her side. 'Oh my god, what is that on your wrist?' I gasped, forgetting she couldn't hear me.

I placed my hand over the scabs forming on her arms and stroked hair. I'd spent many an evening plaiting that hair. I knew almost every strand.

Leanne repeated my action, her hand followed the exact same pattern mine had. I stared at my hand in disbelief, then glanced around her room. It was a mess; clothes were strewn all over the place, and my nose crinkled at a funny smell.

The bin was full of crumpled pieces of paper, all covered in writing and doodles.

A half-eaten pizza in its box was poking out from under the bed.

Long gone where the posters of Lady Gaga and Katy Perry, replaced with bands I'd never even heard of, though they had one thing in common: they all wore black.

One poster stood out to me the most. It read 'Black is my happy colour.'

Blimey, this isn't good, Leanne.

I went back over to her and placed my hands on her shoulders. I could sense she needed my help; she had hurt herself. I knew instinctively it was more than a passing phase.

'Caroline, you don't know what impact you had on my life, and now you're gone. You helped me with my homework, and I really looked up to you,' Leanne sighed, then reached for a bobble to tie her hair back. 'I didn't crave your dress sense back then, even though it had been unique,' she continued. 'You might wonder why I'm talking to you out loud. My mum said it might help me if I spoke to you. She said you might hear me, but I dunno…' She shrugged.

'Oh, that's why I'm here…' I muttered.

'I can't believe you're gone. I'm struggling with college, and I've lost contact with the few friends I had after some petty squabbles,' she said as more tears fell. 'I feel so low these days, and I don't want to be here anymore. I want to be where you are, Caroline.'

'Oh crap.' I knelt beside her again and squeezed her knee. 'You can't talk that way, do you hear me, Leanne? You're still a young girl. I'd give my right arm to be back here with you all. Oh gosh, you can't hear me…'

I scanned the room frantically for something to use to get her attention. I peered on the dresser and focused on the e-reader. 'Please work…' I pleaded.

I scanned the text she'd been reading for a word that may help. I found the word *strong* and pressed it; it highlighted under my touch.

'Look, Leanne, this is what you need to be. It's right here in front of you.'

The word flickered, and she looked down.

'Yes, Leanne, keep looking,' I urged.

'What the…' she whispered and shook her head. 'I'm not strong.'

I pressed the word *beautiful*.

'What's going on?' Leanne said, looking over her shoulder. She moved the page along, as though to erase the highlighted words.

I scanned the new page and highlighted *important*.

'Jeez, what's up with this thing?' She picked it up, studied it, and placed it back down. She glanced in the mirror again and wiped her tears away.

'Yes, Leanne, you're getting this,' I said.

CHAPTER NINE

Then I highlighted the word *wanted*. I had to let her know she was all of those things. She did matter.

'Caroline?' she mumbled. 'Is that you?'

I highlighted *yes*.

'Caroline?' She sniffed. 'I want to be with you. I can't cope here.'

I highlighted every single *no* I could find. I was out of words.

'No?' she asked and cleared all the highlighted words.

I highlighted them again, and she hung her head. After a moment, she broke down into the loudest, uncontrollable sobs I'd ever heard.

I embraced her in a huge bear hug and hoped she felt the comfort I was trying to impart on her. Then I heard someone thumping up the stairs, and the door burst open.

'What is it, Leanne?' her mother said, running to her side.

Leanne bent over and buried her head in her hands.

'Leanne, I can't help you if don't open up to me, love.'

She continued to cry, but silently now.

Her mother stroked her back. 'Do you want me to get some help for you?'

I looked back at the e-reader and highlighted the word *yes*.

Leanne glanced at the screen but didn't move her position. Instead, she spoke to her mother from her reflection in the mirror. 'Yes. I think I do need some help.'

Leanne's mother smiled. 'I'm so pleased you've changed your mind. I've been out of my mind with worry. Come on, how about a glass of milk and a white-chocolate chip cookie? Your favourite.'

'Okay. Be down in a sec. I need to clean myself up a bit.'

I sighed with relief as her mother walked out and closed the door behind her.

'Thank you, Caroline,' whispered Leanne.

She grabbed some tissues, wiped her face, then sighed heavily, causing her breath to steam up the mirror. I drew a love heart quickly for her.

'I'm glad you've asked your mum for help,' I said and highlighted the word *welcome* before I left.

* * *

Speed-dating night arrived, and I was looking forward to meeting new people. Each date would only last a few minutes, and I would be under no obligation to see them again.

I arrived ahead of time for the event, though my eagerness and nerves caused me to land on a little stool when I arrived in the pub. Somehow, the stool toppled over, and I went with it.

My nose was level with a table, and five pairs of eyes stared down at me. I scrambled to my feet and righted the stool on my first attempt, much to my amazement. Then I brushed myself down. My gran's phrase poured out of my mouth: 'Where there's no dust, there's no cobwebs.'

Two older spirits laughed, while the others continued to stare. I dashed off to stand at the bar and hoped I wouldn't bump into them later.

I clocked Jane as I weaved through the other spirits. She also spotted me, leaving her group to head my way.

'Hi, Caz,' said Jane, a smile plastered to her face. 'Okay, you don't mind if I call you Caz, do you?'

Jane's sudden friendliness put me on edge. We hadn't exactly become pals when we first met, and I only allowed my closest friends and family to shorten my name.

'I do mind actually, Jane,' I said. 'My name is Caroline.'

She shrugged. 'Okay, fair enough. I'm glad you came tonight,' she said, keeping up the bizarre pleasantness.

My exterior softened a little. 'Me too. I've never been to one before.'

'Okay, well, I'm sure you'll enjoy it. Listen,' she glanced around, then moved closer to whisper, 'a few of us would like to speak to you after, if that's okay?'

Here we go, I thought. I knew she had to have an ulterior motive.

I shuffled my feet. 'What about?'

'Don't look so worried. We've decided to help you out with your revenge problem.'

'How can *you* help? I thought all I needed was determination.' I rolled my eyes.

'We're going to teach you, okay?'

'Really!' I exclaimed. 'You can truly teach me?'

Two nearby spirits paused their conversation to stare at us.

'Shh! Keep it to yourself,' she said pulling me away. 'But yes, really, okay?'

'I can't wait!' I almost squealed.

'Perfect. I'll come find you afterwards, okay?'

'Sure.'

I could hardly contain my excitement; I hadn't smiled this much in a long time, and I almost skipped as I went to find a better spot near the stage. If Jane and her friends helped me out, then I could deal with Clare, then put her and James behind me. I didn't question Jane's new willingness to help me; it was a welcome change of events. I had learnt bits on my own, and I was sure with their help, I could crank it up a notch.

The pub bustled with spirits from all eras, judging by their attire. There were spirits of all shapes, sizes, and colours, and as I looked around, it reminded me of the game you play when you pick which famous people you would invite to a dinner party, dead or alive. I hoped the variety would make for an interesting night.

I didn't have to wait long for it to start. Frankie G soon made his way onstage to another loud round of applause.

'Please, you are too kind.' Frankie G bowed and laughed. 'Welcome, everyone, to our monthly speed dating night.'

A few eager individuals clapped and whistled.

'All the regulars and *irregulars*,' he winked, 'bear with me while I fill in any newbies. Here's how the night works. You all come up and take a chip from the bowl. A red chip means you stay seated, and yellow chips move from table to table. You get three minutes at each table, then the bell will ring. If you can't select your own chip, just let someone know. There's no shame here; one will be selected for you. Any questions?' he asked and walked to the edge of the stage. The room stayed silent.

'Before I forget, there is no split by gender. You will date all across the spectrum. If anyone has a problem with that, I suggest you leave now,' he snarled. 'We have no time for homophobia in this establishment.'

My mouth hung agape. I would never have pinned Frankie G as an advocate for LGBTQ+ rights. I shook my head in shame. I'd been caught out more than once for judging people. This served me right for not broadening my horizons while I had been living.

My untimely demise had given me the opportunity to get comfortable out of my secure and familiar bubble. To date the

CHAPTER NINE

same gender had never crossed my mind before, but I wanted to be open to it. Even if I didn't make a connection, I might be able to make some new friends.

We all formed a queue and selected our chips. I managed to pick out a red one and found an empty table. There, I tried to compose myself. I looked at the faces around me. Everyone smiled as they took their seats, which eased my nerves a little.

The bell rang, and a large frame sat opposite me, obscuring my view of the pub. My first date called himself Michelle. He informed me he'd spent his days on building sites and his evenings in drag around the clubs in Essex. He wore a huge blonde wig that reminded me of a Texan beauty pageant contestant I'd seen on television and a dress embellished with purple sequins that matched his eyeshadow and lipstick.

In three minutes, he had enthralled me with tales of his escapades, and I told him snippets of my life so far on the spiritual plane. I was saddened to learn he died as a result of a hate crime. Fortunately, the culprits were found and were serving time in prison. It's awful how narrowminded people can be. We promised to meet up another night to continue our conversation.

I exchanged small talk with the next few dates, and though pleasant enough, we didn't have much in common to form a connection.

After the ring of the next bell, Mark sat down. He died at the same age as me on his milk round in the nineties. His float had been crushed by a lorry. I filled him in on my accident. I hadn't thought about the crash in days.

I pulled my bag closer to me as I replayed the police officer's conversation with my dad. *Why didn't James brake?*

'Are you okay, Caroline? You zoned out there,' Mark said

warmly. The concern in his eyes made my stomach flutter; a sensation I thought I'd never experience again.

'Yes, sorry, just talking about the accident… upset me a little.' I smiled sadly.

Mark nodded his understanding; our shared experience meant we had plenty to discuss, and we arranged to meet the following Friday.

The event finished, and my earlier enthusiasm for dating deflated like an old balloon, as I'd only made two connections. But I couldn't stew in my disappointment or self-pity, as Jane and her friends were about to teach me all I needed to know about scaring Clare.

'Caroline!' Jane shouted excitedly. 'Come here,' she beckoned.

My excitement returned, and I almost skipped over in anticipation.

'Did you enjoy it?' she asked.

'Yep, it was alright. I'm eager to get started with my lesson, though.'

'Wonderful. Okay, come with me, there are some people I want you to meet.'

Jane walked towards a door at the side of the stage, and I followed. She rapped on the wood twice, then entered.

'Okay, guys,' Jane said to the occupants of the room, 'this is the woman I was telling you about.'

The room appeared larger than the pub; I couldn't be sure it even belonged to the pub. It looked like a ballroom straight out of a stately home. For all I knew, we'd walked through the door into another dimension.

I spotted cardboard boxes scattered all over and ornaments on the tables. There were pictures of all shapes and sizes hung on the walls, in addition to two full-length mirrors. The room was lit by three huge chandeliers.

'Okay, Caroline, don't be shy. Say hello,' said Jane.

I gave a half-hearted wave and said hello. No one reciprocated my initial greeting, so I dropped my hand awkwardly.

'I'll introduce everyone, okay, then explain what's going to happen.'

'Okay,' I muttered.

'Okay. Jack, you'll remember. I heard you put him in his place.' Jane laughed, but Jack didn't speak. Instead, he tipped his hat in salutation.

Jane continued: 'Benny the T, you've met.'

I nodded at him, and his grin grew wider. I noticed he wore wooden clogs, though as he hadn't spoken, I didn't know his nationality.

'Mary, you know.'

The Scottish redhead also smiled at me.

'Now for the ones you don't know...' Jane turned to the two young women remaining. 'This is Andie.'

'Hey,' said Andie. She briefly looked up, then stared back at her pink shoes dotted with daisies.

'And finally, this is Rosabelle. Her friends call her Rose.'

'Hello,' she said warmly. Rosabelle wore bell-bottomed jeans and a colourful tank top. If I had to guess, I would have said she died in the seventies.

'Okay, introductions out of the way. Mary or Jack, do you want to explain?' said Jane.

'I'll take this one,' said Jack as he walked into the centre of the group. 'Don't hover near the door, Caroline. Come a bit closer, we don't bite.'

I inched forwards. The atmosphere changed, and the air

prickled the hairs on my neck.

'Caroline, you've been told the golden rule is not to draw attention to yourself, and that will remain the party line. But,' Jack held his finger up, 'you can learn to make your presence known. What you learn here must not be shared with anyone outside the group without our prior consent. Do you understand?'

I nodded. 'So, what is this, *Fight Club*?' I smirked.

'A fight club? No, this is serious, Caroline,' Jack snapped. 'Even Frankie G is oblivious to this.'

I guessed they didn't get my little joke. I forgot they all probably came from different decades. And why didn't Frankie G know? I thought he ran this place.

'I'm sorry. Of course, I understand. I'll appreciate anything you can show me.'

'Super. What have you learnt so far? Tell the group,' Jack said, pacing around the room.

'Umm…' I rubbed my hands together, 'I can travel okay now.'

'Well, that's a given. It's the first thing we learn. Anything else?' Jack asked.

'I can hold a book,' I replied.

'Good, that's a start. And?'

'I like opening and closing kitchen cupboards and drawers.'

'Excellent, you've found your speciality,' he said, continuing to pace. 'Now we've got to get you to the next level. It's all well and good doing that, but…' he paused to look at me, 'you don't want your intended target to think he's gone cuckoo or been sleepwalking and raiding the cupboards at night. No. What you need is a scare factor. We've got to get you from opening the cupboards and drawers to pulling the contents out.'

'Do you think you can build up to that, hen?' asked Mary.

CHAPTER NINE

I nodded my head vigorously.

'Super.' Jack clapped his hands. 'We will start small so I can see for myself what you can do.'

'Sure, what do you want me to do?' I asked.

'Can you tilt a couple of the pictures for me?'

I scanned the room. 'I'll try…' I said.

The collective followed as I walked over to a large oil painting. I peeped over my shoulder; six eager faces looked back at me.

Looking back at the ornate golden frame, I tried to push the bottom right corner, but my finger missed.

I dropped my hands to my sides and closed my eyes. This is when I would have normally taken a deep breath.

'This is going to be a long day,' said Jack, not even bothering to whisper for my benefit.

Irritated, I tried again and managed to move the painting by a centimetre.

'It's a start…' said Jack.

'Let me try again,' I said. *And it really doesn't help to have you all standing behind me.*

I moved along to a smaller painting and repeated the process. This time, the frame was clearly crooked.

'That's better,' said Jack. 'Now, how about you flick the light switch on and off. That will give your intended victim a scare.'

I didn't like the way he said victim; it rolled off his tongue in a way that made me want to shudder. I was uncomfortable now. But I had to stay and learn, *didn't I?*

I looked around the room and spotted the light switch near the door we had entered. As I walked over, the group followed again; it was like I had my own fan club.

I found it easy to flick the lights on and off. So much so, I did five times before Jack stopped me.

'That's enough of that now. Caroline, fetch that box over there and bring it to this table,' Jack pointed.

I followed his finger, and my eyes widened. 'I don't think I can. It's too big,' I stammered. I hadn't handled anything as large as that yet; it was the size of Tamara's old birthing ball.

'Try, Caroline,' encouraged Rosabelle.

I sighed and walked over. As I did, I felt the pressure of six pairs of eyes boring into me. I reached for the box, but my hands missed. I paused and tried again. My fingers wouldn't touch it. I grumbled under my breath.

Rosabelle appeared at my side. 'It's alright, I'll bring it over for you.'

Jack tutted as we walked back over.

'I'm sorry, it's just a bit big,' I said.

'No. It's time for a pep talk. The problem, Caroline, is one I see time and time again. Your mind still thinks it's living in the material world. It's not living.' He crossed his arms, but his tone had softened. 'You are dead and residing within the spiritual plane. You are on the other side of alive. You must push through the invisible barrier that exists between our plane and the living one. Once you can do that, you can do anything,' he said.

I nodded my comprehension. Until then, I'd never seen it that way. I had still seen myself as part of the living world, as though I belonged there. I had to work hard to remember my world only looked the same. The normal rules of physics no longer applied.

'It also helps if you can effectively channel an emotion. You need to focus on the one that gets the strongest reaction. Anger usually works best,' said Andie.

CHAPTER NINE

'Okay, let's poke her,' laughed Jane as she walked over to me, fingers poised at the ready.

I moved out of her reach.

'No. You're not poking anybody, Jane. What are you, five?' snarled Jack.

Jane rolled her eyes and stepped back. 'Okay, okay...'

'Caroline, pick an object out of the box and throw it across the room, you dirty, little piss ant!' Jack shouted at me, his chest thrust out.

I edged back towards the door. 'Hey, there's no need for name calling!'

'No time for niceties, tea, and biscuits. You've got to use what triggers you, and work with it. Now, get something out of that box before I knock you into next week.'

I stomped over to the table where Rosabelle had placed the box and peered in. It contained an assortment of trinkets, ornaments, and candles. I focused on an old Victorian brooch and tried to envisage my hand pushing through a barrier to pick it up.

'Okay, what are you waiting for?' Jane shouted. 'Pick it up, pick it up,' she started to chant and clap, and the rest joined in.

The table started to rock.

I clenched my teeth and roughly grabbed the brooch before the moving table dislodged it from its position, then I flung it at the group; it just missed Jane's head.

That'll teach you.

'Bravo!' yelled Jack. 'Anger works like a charm.'

Jane glowered at me and stepped forward. Mary put her arm in front of her, and she inched back.

The table slowed to a gentle shake.

'Try something bigger, Caroline,' Rosabelle coaxed.

'All right,' I said as I returned Jane's glare.

I focused on a lavender candle and replayed the group's chants in my head. I reached for the candle and hurled it at one of the mirrors. The candle bounced off the mirror and landed upright.

'Excellent.' Jack clapped and tipped his hat. 'Now, don't even think about what you're doing. Empty every item out of the box. No hesitation.'

I did as he instructed and pictured Clare's face witnessing the destruction I was going to unleash in her house. I emptied the box in ten seconds flat. 'I did it!' I yelled and punched the air. But just as I had at home, I felt drained and sunk onto a nearby stool.

'Tires you out, doesn't it?' said Andie.

'Yeah, why is that?' I asked.

She shrugged. 'No one knows. Be careful, and rest now and again until you feel totally ready for what you want to do.'

'She's right,' chimed Mary. 'Now, you rest a minute, hen, and we'll show you what we can do.'

I nodded and watched the group spread out.

Mary counted down from three. On one, the group threw and tossed whatever they could get their hands on. I ducked as a table came flying at my head.

'Hey, watch out!' I yelled, but my voice was lost in the bedlam. A sound like wind started to build and intensify, and the air crackled.

I watched on in horror as each of their faces twisted, distorted, and stretched until their faces were unrecognisable, and their figures took on a blue hue.

The group started to dash around the room, almost inflight. I could no longer distinguish between their bodies.

CHAPTER NINE

I knelt down and took cover near a table. A figure dashing through the madness caught my eye; it didn't have the same blue hue as the others. I looked to see where it had gone but was distracted by a member of the group leaping from one chandelier to the next, leaving them swinging in their wake. Then a pair stood juggling with items out of another box.

I searched for the figure again as tables slid up and down the room, and chairs stacked themselves into towers. I didn't need to look far; he had slid in at the other side of the table. It was Daniel. Again.

I opened my mouth to speak, but he indicated for me to be quiet.

Then his voice cut through the crackling air.

'JANE!' he bellowed.

'Get back on your scooter, Daniel,' a voice replied.

I'd seen and heard enough. I tore out of there as fast as I could and smashed into my coffee table as I landed in my living room, sending shards of glass all over the floor.

'Fuck! Shit!' I shouted as I tried to comprehend how I'd managed to break it.

Nothing about the spirit world made sense to me.

I didn't attempt to clean up the mess I had made. I hoped either James or his mother would deal with it. Instead, I went upstairs and lay on the bed. I had no words to express what I'd just witnessed. Jane and her friends had looked like creatures from another world.

And what was with Daniel? Why had he shown up yet again?

Eisen's warning rang in my head. He'd told me to stay away from them, and with good reason, from what I'd seen tonight.

What they had been able to do looked dangerous, and it crossed my mind how many people they had done that too and possibly hurt. Jane had said Daniel had hurt someone, but what if they all had?

I felt bad for Frankie G. He seemed to be respected by most of the punters, despite the underground scare ring being held right under his nose.

With all I had seen, I had a lot of thinking to do.

Chapter Ten

I lay on my bed for over twenty-four hours as I replayed what I'd learnt and seen. Eisen's earlier warning still echoed around my head.

I didn't want to turn into a monster—or whatever Jane and her friends had turned into. But even with that in mind, I was still hellbent on scaring Clare. I'd gone back and forth, back and forth, until I knew I had to take action against her.

My heart and mind wouldn't let it go.

I would just never do it again.

At ten o'clock on Sunday morning, I thought of Clare and arrived in her kitchen. I looked around the area I had to work with; two empty wine glasses sat in the graphite sink, Clare's signature lipstick smeared all over one of them. I wondered if James's lips had sipped from one those glasses or if they only rendezvoused at their little love nest.

A rumour had circulated the office about Clare's love of a monthly subscription service for fresh flowers. I didn't know if the rumour was true, but flowers had been strategically placed on her breakfast bar. A couple of petals had fallen onto the worktop. I thought Clare pretentious for falling for such a gimmick, but I had to admit they looked nice.

I wandered into the living room; the house dripped money.

Clare redecorated this room every two years. She claimed it was the centre of her house and should be kept up to date. The kitchen had been the centre of our house, especially at parties, what little we had.

But what did I know? Compared to me, Clare was what I called a proper grown-up. I threw tantrums when I didn't get my own way, and I drank beer out of the bottle—or at least I used to, my mind reminded me.

Remembering the task at hand, I crept around the rest of the house looking for Clare and arrived in her bedroom. Clothes were laid out neatly on the bed, and the door to the en-suite was closed; behind it came the muffled sound of running water.

Satisfied she was home, I headed back downstairs to make a start. I wanted her to walk into that kitchen and be scared out of her wits.

She had a large kitchen, so I started at the end nearest the living room. I tingled with anticipation as I opened the drawers and cupboards, placing a few items precariously stacked atop each other for maximum effect.

'What are you doing?' A man's voice made me jump. 'Turn around slowly,' he said.

I put my hands up and turned to face him.

He scoffed. 'Put your hands down, you silly girl, I'm not the police.'

The voice belonged to an older gentleman, a fellow spirit. He was shorter than me and a little tubby. He wore a knitted Christmas jumper, brown trousers, and suede moccasins.

'I'm Caroline. I work with Clare.' I shook my head. 'I mean, I used to work with Clare. I died almost a fortnight ago.'

'I asked what you were doing. I didn't ask for your life story,' he retorted.

CHAPTER TEN

'Sorry, well, I'm getting revenge. I'm going to scare her,' I said and flexed my fingers.

'What do you mean, you're getting revenge? And what good is opening a few doors and cupboards, anyhow?' he said, raising one eyebrow.

'I'm not finished yet; this is just the start!' I snapped and moved to the next cupboard.

'No, no, no. Absolutely not. Not in my house!' He waved his arms around manically as he spoke. 'I don't want any of you poltergeist types loitering in my house.'

'Huh, what do you mean?' I asked, half-heartedly continuing my task.

'I don't want any of them crazy blue things floating around my house, causing havoc. They're impossible to reason with when they're in full rage mode, and I won't have it!' he yelled.

'I don't know what you're talking about, but I'm not one of those things,' I said, tilting my chin up.

'You say you aren't now, but trust me, you will be,' he said, shaking his head. 'Once you get into a rampage of moving objects and flying around the room, charging at your intended victim, there'll be no stopping you. The buzz you will get is addictive. You'll want to do it all the time.'

I paused midway through opening the cutlery drawer. 'Are you serious?'

The confidence I'd had evaporated.

'As serious as the heart attack that put me here.' He sniffed. 'You'll never be who you were if you do this,' he warned. 'It's evil, and there's no coming back.'

I sat on a nearby stool. It all made sense now. Why Eisen had warned me away from Jane and her friends. On the surface, they didn't seem evil; it's surprising what lingers beneath, waiting to burst out. Eisen had tried to steer me away from this path.

I didn't want to be evil. I wanted to be me.

'Caroline you said your name was, right?' the man said, interrupting my thoughts.

'Yes.'

'Why do you want to scare Clare if you worked with her?'

'Pure and simple revenge.'

The man's eyebrows raised, then he smiled. 'I'm intrigued. I've not spoken to anyone in a long time. Why don't you come sit with me in the living room and tell an old man your story?'

'Okay…' I said slowly, 'but you have to tell me your name first.'

'I'm sorry, where're my manners?' He brought a hand to his forehead. 'I'm George. That's what you get for keeping to yourself for so long.'

'Nice to meet you, George.' I hopped off the stool and walked towards George and the living room.

'Tsk, tsk,' he said and wagged his finger as I approached. 'Are you forgetting something?' He pointed at the kitchen.

'Oh… guess I should shut everything and put things back.' I laughed sheepishly as I started to return the items and close the cupboards and drawers as quickly as I could.

'Softly, softly, catchee monkey,' he said. 'Can't have you getting riled up.'

I heeded George's warning and slowed down. I finished, and we sat in the living room on a huge, grey crushed-velvet sofa.

'How do you know about those blue things?' I asked him. 'Poltergeists, you called them.'

'Seen 'em for myself, ain't I? That's why I stopped going out. Too many strange things out there for my liking. Much better if I just stay here and watch the world pass me by.' He sighed and looked towards the window.

'Don't you get lonely?'

'Not really. I have my memories to keep me company. I won't be here for much longer, anyway. Michael will be coming to collect me soon and then I'll be reunited with my dear wife. It's not too bad here, except for the trollop upstairs.' He pointed to the ceiling.

'Trollop?' I laughed. 'That's one word for her,' I said, eyeing the room. It shouted money but poor taste. Like someone who had just won millions and bought every expensive item in the shop.

'Do you know she redecorates every two years?' George said. 'I couldn't believe it when they took down my flocked wallpaper. It was a lovely maroon colour. I don't know why she bothers; it's not to my taste at all.'

'I know she does.' I laughed. 'I mean, who does she think she is?' I got up and crossed to an ugly painting mounted above the TV. 'Look at this. It's a Picasso gone wrong, don't you think so?'

'I know nothing about art,' he said with a wave of his hand. 'Right, Caroline, no use skirting round it. Tell me why you feel the need to get revenge and what for?'

I liked George. He made me feel at ease, and I could talk to him about my problems. He reminded me of my grandfather on my dad's side.

I explained to him how I had found out about the affair, the time I'd spent on my own trying to learn things, and the incident at The Lion's Head.

'You've had a busy couple of weeks, but do you really think revenge is the best course of action?' he eyed me intensely.

'You could be doing so much more with whatever time you've got left. You're young, go see the world! Spend time with like-minded people.'

'Well, I was going to forge a path for myself afterwards, and I thought I'd met like-minded people at The Lion's Head,' I said glumly.

George shook his head. 'Stay away from there. Frankie G doesn't know what's going on under his nose. He may have the bravado that everything is fine and dandy, but God forbid what would happen in that place if he found out.' He shook his head again.

'You've been there?' I asked.

'Sure. I accidentally stumbled upon the crazy blue poltergeists in the backroom. I wanted no part of it. Once the rage and anger consumes you, any little thing can set you off—or so I've been told. And like I said, you won't be the same person in here,' he said, putting a hand over his heart.

'Okay, I think I understand. I just don't want *her* to have him. Is that stupid of me?' I let my gaze fall to where my hands messed with the bottom of my t-shirt.

'I know, dear, but listen to an old man who knows things. Clare will never get to keep him. Clare is a very private person, so I'll tell you something you might not know. She bought this house after my wife died, *and* she was married—nice man, too. And do you know how many times she has been married since?'

I frowned. 'No. How many?'

'Another two times, would you believe!' he exclaimed.

I gasped.

'Wow, I never knew that.' I scanned the room again with new eyes. There weren't any pictures of any men—or Clare,

CHAPTER TEN

for that matter. 'I thought she'd just been married the once,' I said.

'I've watched Clare, and the problem with her is she wants what everybody else has. She likes it for a year or two, then she gets shut of it. Same with men. She's done it with every man I've seen in this house. If she acted like that in my day, she'd have been sent straight to the workhouse,' he laughed. 'That was a joke. I'm not that old, but you get the gist.'

'Sure. She must be truly miserable inside.'

I thought I knew Clare but everything thing about her was a front. She was a complete stranger to me.

George shrugged. 'I don't know about that, I'm no psychologist. All I know is she always seems to be on the hunt for her next victim. No doubt she was jealous of your marriage, so she inserted herself into James's life and took him for herself.'

The word victim sent a shiver through me, but not for the same reason it had with Jack. I felt like a victim, and not just because Clare stole my man. I was a victim of an unjust, early death.

'I'm not so sure about that, George. I've had doubts about how strong our marriage was. There had to be a reason he could be taken so easily,' I sighed.

'Don't batter yourself needlessly. Marriage is a sacred vow. I'm a firm believer in talking through the problems and not running into the arms of someone else.' He smiled.

'Thank you, George.' I forced a smile. 'I appreciate you trying to make me feel better.'

'You are very welcome,' he said and patted my arm.

George's revelations had surprised me. Clare always had the persona of a happy person, but it was all a lie. The news made me realise that you never know what's going on behind closed doors.

I knew then I had to leave her be. Even if she married James, I'm sure he'd be gone in a year or two.

A noise on the stairs startled me.

'Is that Clare?' I asked.

'Yes, we best move. You go stand in that corner, and I'll go over there.' He pointed to the opposite corner.

'You don't stand in the corner all the time, do you, George?'

'No.' He frowned. 'I usually move from room to room and stay out of her way.'

'Did you see me earlier, then?'

'Sure, I did. I kept an eye on you from where you couldn't see me until I could make sense of what you were up to.' He laughed.

At that moment, Clare waltzed into the room dressed in a bright-pink kimono and teddy bear slippers. She sprawled out on the sofa and switched on the television.

I had the urge to fly across the room at her, but I sensed George's eyes boring into me, warning against it. He took my mind off her by telling me what this spirit life was like for him.

I learnt spirits could come back now and again, even if they had chosen to move straight up. Our connection with the living world wasn't totally behind us.

My heart broke for George when he described the shock he felt when he realised his wife, June, had decided to go straight up and never came back to visit. He told me he'd been sure she would come back.

He had tried to make his presence known in subtle ways; he didn't go full on poltergeist, as he called it. He moved a couple of items, got into bed with her on an evening...

He described his theories on why old people sometimes

CHAPTER TEN

smell, not in a nasty way, but because spirits get into bed with them, and it makes them sweat during the night. I recalled how my mother had been hot when I cuddled into the small of her back in bed.

I guessed June had either chosen to ignore the signs, or she didn't believe what she'd seen or felt. Either way, George forgave her for not coming back, and he couldn't wait to be reunited.

I eyed Clare as she got up and shimmied into the kitchen.

Two seconds later, her voice interrupted our conversation.

'What the?' she exclaimed.

George and I ran into the kitchen to find Clare stood in front of an open cupboard.

'Oops,' I muttered. 'Guess I missed one.'

George shook his head. 'Never mind, I'm sure she'll get over it. She'll probably think she left it open last night.'

I didn't share George's confidence. Clare was meticulous. Not one thing was out of place.

She stood staring at it for several minutes, then shook her head and closed it.

I shrugged, and we went back to our respective corners.

A loud pounding on the front door startled the pair of us.

'Who's that? They're going to put the door through,' I said.

George frowned and walked to the window. 'Oh, not this great lump again.'

I joined him at the window as Clare whizzed past us and ran upstairs. Then we heard a door slam.

'I know you're in there!' the brutish man shouted through the letterbox.

'Do you know who it is George?'

He shrugged. 'Just a scorned ex-lover is my guess.'

The man pounded at the door again, even louder this time.

'We had an arrangement, Clare!' he yelled.

Now, that didn't sound like something a jilted lover would say. But he eventually gave up and walked off. Clare remained wherever she was hiding.

'Can I ask you something else, George?' I asked after we'd drifted back to our corners.

'Of course, you can, Caroline. I think we're firm friends, now, don't you?'

I smiled. 'Yes, I do believe we are.' I paused, then asked, 'Why are you wearing a Christmas jumper?'

He placed his hand over the reindeer. 'This? I chose not to change my clothes. June knitted this, and she gave it to me the morning I died.'

'Oh, George, how awful on Christmas Day.'

'I don't think my body could cope with all the food. I should have become a vegetarian or one them vegans,' he laughed and pointed at my t-shirt.

I laughed too. I didn't have the heart to tell him I hadn't been a vegetarian.

Meat is Murder was one of my favourite albums. I could never give up meat. I liked Sunday roasts too much—especially my mum's.

'Is there anything else you can tell me about the spirit world, George?' I looked at him eagerly. I felt I could trust any information he could give me.

'You know, I don't go out much...' He paused and stroked his chin. 'But I can tell you about robins.'

'Robins?' I said, looking to the window.

'Yes, robins. It is my understanding that a robin is designated to each person who has passed. When a person sees a robin, it

CHAPTER TEN

means their loved one is watching over them.' He smiled.

'Huh,' I said, wondering how that would work.

'But sometimes, they get too busy, and that's why you should have a supply of white feathers,' he continued.

'What do I need feathers for?'

'Anytime you see a loved one, leave a feather. They will know you have been close by.'

'Okay, where can I get some?' I asked.

'You can have mine,' he said. 'I've nobody left to give them to, anyway.'

George walked over from his corner and handed me a pile of fluffy white feathers from his pocket. I tucked them away safely in my handbag.

'Thank you, George. Where do the feathers come from?'

'You're welcome. Oh, hmm... I don't really know.' He shrugged. 'I like to believe they come from the angels. I didn't see any wings on them, though, did you?'

'No, I don't believe I did,' I said, thinking back.

A creak on the landing preceded the soft padding of feet down the staircase.

'I think it's time you be off now,' George said.

I nodded as Clare returned. She looked frightened as she hid behind the heavy curtains to peek out the window. He definitely wasn't some scorned lover.

Chapter Eleven

Monday came around again, two weeks since I'd returned. I could never go back to The Lion's Head, and that meant my budding friendships with Michelle and Mark were over before they'd even began.

I'd been lucky to meet George, though. He'd saved me from becoming something I had no taste for. If I'd gone down that road, it would have been the end for me as the person I knew.

But now I had no plan in place and nowhere to go. I had to start all over again. And the day didn't help my woes; I hated Mondays, and to top it off, I had the distinct feeling I had been pushed underwater, and my spirit was fighting to get back to the surface.

I half expected to be pulled away any minute with the way my stomach rolled, but nothing happened.

I left the house and walked to the local supermarket for a change of scenery and in the hope I might come across some other spirits.

The store had automatic doors, and I slipped in with the other shoppers.

The morning rush meant it was busy, and the store was large; it sold clothes and electric items, as well as groceries and household goods. I used to flick through the magazines before I did my shopping. I couldn't do that anymore unless I wanted to send shoppers running for the exits.

I browsed the clothes and underwear, then made my way to the far end of the store to look at the wine. I had always liked wine but had no clue what to buy. If it tasted good and didn't give me a banging head and a flip-flop tongue the next day, then it suited me fine.

I froze at the entrance to the aisle when I glimpsed a familiar figure perusing the bottles of red: Clare.

The anger I'd pushed down the day before rose to the surface. I know I promised George I'd leave her alone, but if I had to believe spirits and the afterlife were real, then I could believe in fate too. I had to be careful and not take things too far. I was sure the supermarket owners wouldn't have been impressed if a demented spirit started flying around the store.

No other shoppers were in the aisle, but I double checked before I stormed over and gave her trolley a firm push.

The look on her face as she watched it careen away from her was priceless; how I wished I could have taken a picture.

She retrieved the trolley, checked the wheels, then carried on.

She kept glancing over her shoulder as she wandered the store, eventually turning down the cereal aisle. I followed.

This aisle had other shoppers, but I didn't care.

As she reached for a box of cornflakes, I knocked half a dozen off the shelf. Her face turned scarlet as the other shoppers rubbernecked, watching and tutting as she scrambled to pick them up. I had never seen her so flustered as she half ran to the next aisle.

I wanted to do more, and my spirit form tingled as it waited for my next move; my confidence and ability grew with each action.

I swiped a shelf containing ready-salted crisps to the floor as Clare swept past it. The entire thing collapsed into the aisle, blocking her trolley from moving farther. I laughed wickedly. There was no stopping me now, and I screamed like a banshee as I flew towards Clare.

But something blocked my way.

'You've got to stop this, Caroline!' it said.

I couldn't focus on the figure. All I saw was Clare's face dancing in front of my eyes.

I shook my head in an effort to focus.

'What's happening to me?' I mumbled.

'It's okay. I'll help you,' he said.

I hesitated and blinked several times, trying to concentrate on the person in front of me despite the magnet trying to pull me in Clare's fleeing direction.

'Daniel?' I gulped.

'Yes, it's me. Everything will be okay. What has she done to you?' he sighed and reached for my hand.

I didn't know which 'she' he was referring to, but I hadn't forgotten Jane's warning, even if I no longer trusted her, either.

'Get away from me!' I yelled and pushed him out of my way.

His face crumpled, and I ran to look for Clare. I had to see what damage I had done.

I found her at the checkouts, her usual flawless complexion was flushed, and the redness had spread down her neck and onto her chest.

What have I done?

I had lost control for a split second. If Daniel hadn't stopped me, god knows what would have happened next.

Daniel. How had he found me again? He had a way of

tracking me down when I least expected it.

Why can't he stay away from me?

I waited for Clare as she packed and paid for her shopping.

I knew I could control myself now. I didn't want to be on the edge of that precipice ever again. George had been right; there would be no coming back from whatever that was.

I continued to follow her as she went to the toilets. Instead of the ladies', she stumbled into the disabled ones. *The nerve*, I thought to myself and snook in before the door closed.

Clare put her shopping bags on the floor and rummaged in her handbag for her phone. Her hand shook as she called someone.

'Oh, I've had the most horrid morning,' she groaned.

I couldn't catch the other person's replies, but it was a male voice on the other end.

'I'm in the supermarket,' she replied.

'Yes, just grabbing a few bits for tonight. You won't believe this, but my trolley went flying down the aisle as if someone had pushed it…'

'It's not funny. I'm serious!'

'No, it wasn't a prank there was no one there—'

'Of course, I checked the bloody wheels.'

'Well, that's not the worst part. I went to pick up a box of cereal and loads of them fell off the shelf. I didn't even touch them.'

'Listen, Steven, I'm not kidding, and that wasn't the worst of it. I think someone is following me.'

I stepped back and collided with the door. She had yet another man on the go. I couldn't believe she had abandoned James already.

'Well… Oh, I don't know what I mean,' Clare said, pacing

the floor.

'Yes. I'll come round after I've been to the hospital,' she sighed.

So, she is still visiting him, then!

'Of course. I still need to visit the poor sap. He's got no one else now. Plus, we need the money.'

'We? Money?' I whispered. *James doesn't have any money... Does he?*

'Listen, *dear brother*, if I don't get my hands on the money, he promised me, we'll be bankrupt quicker than you can say "tax man."'

Brother? What brother?

I'd heard enough. I flushed the toilet and ran out; the door slammed against the wall as I left. I took a quick glance over my shoulder and saw Clare stood there, dumbstruck. Her handbag and its contents had spilled onto the floor.

As I walked home, I wavered between pangs of guilt at breaking my promise to George and anger at Clare for wanting to get her claws on James's money.

The money that I was completely in the dark about. And how did Clare know?

I couldn't even begin to comprehend what the pair of them had been cooking up being my back.

James had a secret pot of money stashed away somewhere.

My whole marriage had been a sham.

A lie.

I realised coming back wasn't all it had cracked up to be with all the rules and dangers. I could lose myself and possibly hurt the people around me.

My marriage had been filled with secrets and betrayal… I was beginning to think coming back was a big mistake.

CHAPTER ELEVEN

And what was with Daniel?

'Daniel?'

He was in my path yet again. His parka gently wafted behind him in the breeze. I didn't know what he was up to, but he was stood in front of a couple of people sat on a bench.

I wanted to confront him, find out why he was showing up every place I went.

'Daniel, what are you doing? Why are you always—'

I reached his side. The woman on the bench had blood trickling down her face while another woman was pressing a jumper to her head. It had to be hers; she only had a satin camisole on. A discarded bicycle lay on a patch of grass nearby.

I brought my hand to my mouth and looked up at Daniel. His eyes grew wide at the sight of my reaction.

'Oh! No, no, no.' He waved his hands. 'Caroline, this is not what it looks like.'

I shook my head as I backed away. 'Jane was right about you. Stay away from me!' I shouted as I turned and vanished.

I arrived home and dropped onto the sofa. It seemed Jane had been right about Daniel, and though I was grateful for his intervention—without him, who knows where or what I would be now—I still didn't want him showing up unexpectedly. Especially after what I had just seen.

I still felt iffy and not because of what I'd done or found out. Something about the day was off. I should have listened to George; he had been right about me being on the edge of turning into a spiteful and vengeful poltergeist.

I sighed, and just as I was about to grab a book to read, my stomach flipped, and the unknown force pulled me from the safety of my living room.

I landed in the middle of a church. Men and woman

streamed in, dressed in black.

Oh god! I'm at a funeral.

I walked down an empty pew and moved to the side to watch the mourners, only to discover I recognised a few people. My stomach sank to my knees when I realised I'd been pulled in to witness my own funeral; no wonder I'd been feeling off all day.

I hadn't even thought about my funeral until that moment. I knew my dad had spoken to a priest, but that was it.

I spotted the huge frame of Uncle Terry hunting for a seat.

'What's he doing here?' I muttered.

My mother had banned him from all family gatherings after he had people in stitches at my wedding. He loved to make up his own words to hymns—usually rude ones.

'Shh, haven't you any respect,' a tiny voice growled behind me.

I knew the voice anywhere.

'Gran?' I turned and ran into her arms. She hugged me close. 'Gran, what are you doing here?'

'Dead or alive, I would never miss my favourite granddaughter's funeral,' she said with a faint smile.

I rolled my eyes. 'Gran, I'm your only granddaughter. I never thought I'd see you again. I've so many questions. And where's Grandad?' I hugged her again and breathed in scent; she still smelt of lavender and butterscotch. I held her at arm's length and took in the sight of her. She looked just as I remembered. Her silver hair perfectly coiffed, and a hint of sparkle in her hazel eyes. She wore a long cashmere cardigan and coral trousers—much nicer than the frumpy dress my father had chosen to bury her in.

'Oh, your grandad doesn't like to visit. Now, it doesn't mean

CHAPTER ELEVEN

he doesn't love you or your dad, he just prefers there to be a finality to death.'

I nodded. 'I understand.'

'And I know you have a lot of questions, but we will talk afterwards.'

'Gran, I really don't feel comfortable paying respects to myself.' I bit my lip but didn't cry; I still hadn't been able to, no matter how hard I tried.

'Time to pull up your big-girl pants, Caroline.'

I laughed; Gran always knew how to lighten the mood.

'This day isn't about you now,' she continued. 'You've been drawn here to provide comfort to your family and friends. And I'll be here to support you.'

I grabbed her hand and squeezed it tight as I scanned the church; almost every pew was full of mourners in the tiny church. 'I can't believe I'm dead…'

'I know, sweetheart. And I don't like to say it, but you just weren't meant to live a long life.'

I looked down into her smiling face. I could always tell when she was lying. 'I know you don't believe that.'

'I'm sorry, love, I could never lie to you. I'm trying to make you feel better. At least you don't have to be with James, anymore. I never liked him, anyway.'

'Hmm, you know what he's been up to, then?'

'Of course. I've been watching over you. I may not have visited often, but you were always at the top of my list. Look, the service is starting,' she said, nodding towards the priest.

My gran led me to the back of the church. I didn't want to be here and witness my own funeral. Nonetheless, having my grandmother at my side helped. Many of the mourners had to be friends and neighbours of my parents, as I didn't recognise half of them.

'I can't believe Mum let Uncle Terry come,' I whispered to my gran. 'He's only going to offend someone or set people off laughing.'

'Now, now, Caroline, you can't ban people from church,' she scolded.

I shook my head, and we watched for a short time. I looked over the faces, some respectfully blank and others more visibly distressed. Then another figure caught my eye; a woman stood to the side, dressed in black with a small veil over her face.

'Who's that over there?' I pointed.

Gran looked, then scoffed. 'Oh, for goodness' sake, that's a lurker.'

I had no time to ask about lurkers before she shouted across the church.

'Oi, lurker!' she yelled.

I gasped and looked around to check no one had heard. The woman turned her head and stared at us. She freaked me out the way she moved, her eyes snapping to us like an owl's to a mouse.

'Yes, I'm talking to you. Get out of here. Now.' Gran gestured with her thumb.

The woman didn't hesitate to leave. She may be little, but no one argued with my gran.

'Gran, you can't do that,' I said, horrified. 'You said people can't be banned from church.'

'Lurkers aren't people. She had no right attending your funeral.'

'What's a lurker, anyway?'

'Well, I don't know their real name. I made it up, but they lurk around grief. They attend funerals and the like, soaking

CHAPTER ELEVEN

up grief like vultures. I think they feed on it.'

I mouthed a silent 'Oh.' My brain felt like mush; I'd been bombarded with too much information in such a short time.

The spiritual world may have looked like the world I'd left, but it had many variations of spirits. When I made the decision to return, I never thought I'd have to deal with poltergeists, lurkers, and lost souls. I'd thought all spirits would be carbon copies of their former selves.

We listened to the rest of the service in silence. My parents had chosen to have me cremated, which shocked me. I supposed it never crossed their minds they would be burying a child. A pile of ashes is all that remained of my twenty-five years on Earth. I'd left no part of me behind: no children, no legacy, no mark, or stamp. Would my friends even remember me in five years' time, I wondered.

The service finished, and we watched the mourners file out. I spotted several of my friends. It pleased me they had made the journey up to the Lake District. My friend Dawn looked pale and washed out; in fact, she appeared to be devastated. Her husband had to hold her up to stop her collapsing. I promised myself I'd go visit once night fell.

'Caroline, go and see your parents. Whisper a kind word and touch them both gently on the shoulder,' Gran instructed.

'Gran, do I have to?' I groaned. 'I want to spend time with you.'

'Go on, do as I say. I know they're coping well. You made the right decision spending your first week with them; it really helped. But just because they haven't drawn you in, it doesn't mean they don't need you to visit. So, remember my advice; it will serve you well to stop by now and again,' she said while gently pushing me towards them.

'Okay, okay…'

I avoided the last of the mourners as I sauntered over to my parents where they spoke quietly to the priest. I whispered to my mother how much I loved her and how proud she made me and placed a feather in her pocket. I repeated the action with my father, whispering for him to take care of Mum and that I loved him very much.

When I'd finished, my gran led me outside, and we walked arm in arm towards some oak trees. As we walked, my stomach turned, and we exited an entirely different cluster of trees, these ones willow, into a familiar graveyard.

'Gran, have you taken me somewhere else?' I asked.

'Yes, dear.'

'Have you brought me here to make me feel guilty? I'm sorry I didn't visit you as often as I should have. Life got in the way. I always thought of you,' I rambled as we walked amid the headstones.

We came to a halt in front of my grandmother's grave.

'No, don't talk wet. That grave isn't me. Memories are more important than mourning me. I have brought you here to remind you of that for when you are thinking about those who are mourning you. I want you to promise me you will check in on everyone you love at least once a week.'

'I promise I will, Gran.' I looked at the faces of the few people visiting their loved ones graves. 'Do you miss being here? Alive, I mean.'

'Not at all, dear, it was getting boring,' she laughed. 'Life just wasn't the same as it used to be. You'd just started your life. I was going to more funerals than weddings. And call me old-fashioned if you like, but I don't like the way the world has changed. I used to love the TV soaps; they used to be light-

CHAPTER ELEVEN

hearted and comical, but now they make us regular folk out to be boozehounds with no substance. Not everyone lives their lives in a pub,' she remarked.

I hummed. We had that in common; I never liked the soaps, either.

Gran patted my hand. 'And do you know what else? I learnt technology slowed the world down. Everything has slowed. Life should be simple, but it's got complicated. It could be so straightforward if people averted their eyes from their little screens. People have forgotten to be nice to each other. You know, I taught you to be kind and truthful.' She beamed at me.

'I know, and I've always tried to follow your advice. Honest, I have.'

'I know, dear, you're a good girl.' She reached up and stroked my cheek like she did in my younger days. 'And one last thing: a little hug and a smile takes the stresses away.'

I laughed. 'No offence, Gran, but you are old-fashioned, and I can't hug anyone anymore...not how I'd like, anyway.'

'You can, Caroline. The living only need to believe your spirit is around, and they will sense you. Did you never sense me at all?'

I breathed in her familiar scent again. 'I thought I did... I could smell you sometimes when I was alone, and I thought of you.' I sighed.

'There you go, then. It's not your fault if the people you love don't believe in life after death. And I know I'm old-fashioned, but they are my views, and I'm sticking to them...' She paused. 'But in all seriousness, Caroline, I was ready to leave. I know you weren't. You must find someone to spend your time with while you're here.'

'So others keep telling me...' I rolled my eyes. 'I would rather stay with you. I seem to be meeting the unsavoury types.'

She tsked. 'Comes with the territory, I'm afraid. You can't stay with me; I'm only a visitor,' she said sadly.

'Okay. I am learning, though. I'm sure I'll meet a few good ones soon.' I chewed on my lip. But I couldn't dwell on that right now; I had my Gran's company. I wobbled my head. 'Can I ask you some questions now?'

'Of course, Caroline, you've got me all afternoon.'

I rubbed the back of my neck; I wasn't exactly sure how to approach the subject, so I just blurted it out. 'Why did you go to London when you were younger?'

She frowned, then sighed. 'I guess it's okay to tell you now. I didn't go out of choice, Caroline. My parents sent me away because I fell in love with a coloured boy.' She sighed again, and her shoulders relaxed as though a weight had been lifted.

'Wow, did you really? Were you a bit of a rebel? Did Grandad know?' My mouth hung open as she answered.

She laughed and her eyes sparkled like they had when she told me stories when I was younger. 'I guess I was a rebel back then, and your grandad knew. I had to be honest with him; he wasn't my first love, but I never told your father. You see, it was almost unheard of for a white to marry outside their race. Your great-grandparents were furious. I swear I saw smoke blow out of my father's ears.' We laughed, then she continued as we weaved up and down the paths between the headstones: 'It was either go to London to live with my spinster aunt and forget about him, or they would disown me. I couldn't face not having my parents in my life. Times have changed now.'

'Did you ever see him again?'

'Who, Phil? Yes, once. A few years later, I was pushing your father in his pram down the precinct, and I saw him go in the fishing tackle shop. He smiled and nodded at me. I think he understood why I left. He was a family man, too.'

'Do you regret leaving?' I asked tentatively.

'No. You should never regret the decisions you make or dwell on them. Do you regret marrying James now you know what he's been doing?' she enquired.

'No, I don't think so…We had some good times,' I said, remembering when we first dated.

'Good.'

Gran started to drift off the path to walk over the graves. I gasped and stopped.

'Gran, what are you doing? Isn't that disrespectful?'

'To who? We are part of this world, Caroline. Come here,' she beckoned. 'Stand beside me and take a look around. Tell me what you see.'

I walked over but was careful where I stood, then did as she asked and inspected the graveyard. There were endless rows of headstones; some had fresh flowers arranged in front of them, others, the flowers had decayed. Considering how large it was, only a handful of people were visiting.

'Well?' she said.

'I only see graves and flowers.' I took a second glance, wondering what else she expected me to see.

'Exactly!' she exclaimed. 'The spirits aren't sitting on top of their headstones, waiting for their loved ones to show up. Can you imagine if this place were full of spirits, it would be like a festival—like that Glastonberry.'

I chuckled at her comparison. 'It's Glastonbury, Gran.'

'Hmm, yes, that. My point is, don't be hanging around these places for too long waiting for someone to bring you flowers.' She bent down and straightened a blue teddy that had fallen over. 'That being said, it doesn't mean they shouldn't be kept looking nice.'

'Um... okay.' I hung behind as my gran continued her path over the graves. It made me think of Eisen and choosing the right path. For now, I was happy to stick with the concrete path beneath my feet.

'Take a gander at this headstone,' she said, stopping in front a granite headstone. 'Now, this guy had a sense of humour,' she sniggered.

I gazed over her shoulder. Under the man's name it read, '*I told you this would happen!*'

I smiled, but I couldn't see the funny side. It only made me wonder if my parents would erect one for me, even though they had me cremated.

'Anything else you want to know, love?' Gran asked, sensing my change in demeanour.

'I don't know,' I sighed and sat on a bench. 'Coming back has been difficult. I thought I was coming back to a world I knew, but it's been blown apart by James and other discoveries. You know, in my first week here, I almost got swept away and then the other day, I nearly turned into one of them poltergeist thingies.'

'The what?' she said, pursing her lips as she sat beside me.

'The blue spirits with twisted faces.'

'Oh, them. Why do you think you were going to turn into one of them?'

'A spirit I met told me. He said if I lost control of my rage in the name of revenge, I'd become one of them, and there would be no coming back from it...' I trailed off.

'Oh, Caroline, I don't think you'll be one of them. I've never seen you lose control of your anger, even when you were

CHAPTER ELEVEN

having a tantrum.' She laughed. 'You can still use what you've learnt. You just need to use it for good, that's all.' She took my hand.

'What do you mean?' I asked.

'What I mean is if someone loses their keys or glasses, find it for them, and put it where they can find it, or steer them in the right direction when you think someone is getting off-track. Never use your abilities for anything other than good, and you will not be like those spirits.'

I raised an eyebrow. 'Are you sure?'

'I'm positive.'

'But the other spirits I met said I had to be angry to access the most power,' I stated.

'Nonsense,' she scoffed. 'All you need is love,' she said, taking both of our hands and placing them over my heart.

I hung my head. 'Gran, if spirits can help the living out, why didn't you help me with James's affair?'

'There was nothing I could do about it, Caroline. I always believed you were on the cusp of finding out. If it hadn't been for "the accident,"' she air-quoted.

I cocked my head. 'Why do you say it like that?'

'Caroline, I was there. He should have braked. Why did he not brake?'

I shook my head. 'I don't know, Gran. I really don't.'

We got up and continued to walk in silence. After we had walked around the entire graveyard, I noticed something peculiar.

'Gran,' I whispered.

'Yes, dear.'

'I don't want to alarm you, but there is a spirit over there with no face…' I whispered. 'And she looks to have mittens where her fingers should be.'

'No need to panic, they won't hurt you.'

'Why is her face missing and where are her fingers?'

'I'll tell you what I've been told,' Gran explained, 'though no one really knows for sure. Once a spirit's family and friends have gone, there is no one left to remember them—unless they are famous. So, inevitably, they forget who they were and what they looked like. Then their faces slowly disappear. I don't know about their fingers. It only happens if they are here for an exceptionally long time,' she said, leaving my side to look at the headstones again.

'Jeez, that's awful. Isn't there anyone that can help her?' I asked the back of her head.

'I don't know, dear. I blame the angels, myself,' she said, engrossed with inspecting the headstones.

'Why?' I asked, intrigued.

'Well, you see, not everyone is as fortunate as you and me.' I watched as my gran dropped to her knees and swept away the moss from the bottom of a headstone. I quickly checked over my shoulder to ensure no one was in our vicinity. 'Some spirits don't even get the opportunity to move up,' she continued. 'Many are left here, trapped, as the angels argue over their fate. Others get given ridiculous amounts of years back here—it's no wonder they lose themselves. Some die so cruelly they cling on and resist being pulled away. They're the ones I feel most sorry for,' she said, shaking her head.

'I'll be giving Michael a piece of my mind when he collects me…' I muttered.

I went over and helped her to her feet.

'You do that. But it won't change anything.' She looked around as though checking for someone. 'There have been

CHAPTER ELEVEN

rumblings, as though something is shifting in our world.'

I nodded. It wasn't the first time this had been mentioned. Eisen had asked me if I felt anything was different. I couldn't give him an answer; how would I know? I hadn't been here more than five minutes in the grand scheme of things.

Gran sighed. 'Caroline, our time is up. I've got to go back now.'

'Aww, Gran, that's not fair. There's still loads we need to talk about.'

'Don't start that, Caroline, I've told you before, your tantrums don't wash with me.'

'Please, Gran,' I whined.

'Come now, don't make this harder than it has to be. I'll see you again.'

Then she hugged me tight and left.

The graveyard seemed a lot creepier now she had gone. It felt as though I had a hundred eyes staring straight at me, though those who lurked had no faces. I had to think if there was something I could do to help.

I ran all the way home.

I'd got into the habit of going in the backdoor of my house, so as to not draw attention to myself. As I walked around the side of the house, a huge black cat rolled around on the lawn, making the most of the April sun. When I got closer, it jumped and hissed at me. I recoiled and hit the wheelie bin. I don't know if the cat had seen me or just sensed my presence in its vicinity.

I had always questioned if animals had a sixth sense and could see things we couldn't ever since my mum brought a stray dog home when I was sixteen.

Josie had been a fluffy gentle giant; we had no idea how old she was or what she had been through, yet she settled into our family in an instant. She always loved to be at the centre of attention, and she had to have someone stroking her at all times. She slept on the end of my bed, despite my father's forbiddances.

We had no issues except now and again, she would wake up in the middle of the night to growl and bark at the ceiling in the corner of my bedroom. I'd turn the light on and find nothing there. It would take ages to calm her down.

After each occurrence, I'd ask my mother if she thought Josie could see something we couldn't, and she thought it might be a possibility, but my father insisted Josie had issues because of her troubled former life. Now I knew she had seen something and probably not something good.

I waited a few hours to give my friend Dawn a chance to get home. I had never seen her so distraught as I had at my funeral.

I thought of Dawn and arrived in her bedroom. She lay sprawled on the bed, asleep, still dressed. I climbed on beside her and gave her a hug. I whispered in her ear that I was okay and left a feather on her pillow, hoping she would know I'd placed it there.

For a while longer, I lay with her, listening to the sounds of her house and her breathing. I could hear her boys laughing at the television downstairs and bickering over who would get the last piece of chocolate. I stayed there until her husband went to bed, then I went home alone.

Chapter Twelve

The time I spent with my grandmother had enlightened me, and although I'd ended up back at square one with no friends on this side of alive and no idea what to do next, I hoped my time here would be fulfilled by good deeds.

I continued to use my home as a base to return to, though I couldn't decide if I should find a new one. James would have to return at some point, and if Clare tagged along in search of the money she needed, then I had to distance myself from her.

After returning from Dawn's, I continued to make my way through the pile of books I'd always insisted I'd get too, while I thought about what I would do next.

I had a lot to ponder: the cause of my accident and the change in the spirit world.

I stayed on my bed until the next day when a familiar sensation grabbed me, and I was pulled from the safety of my bed and placed into a strange room.

I immediately stepped back into the nearest corner to assess my new environment.

Tamara sat at a large table with a man opposite her; he wore heavily tinted glasses, and his hair was dusted with grey.

He had a small wooden box in front of him, fashioned to resemble a medieval book. Next to the book sat a stack of yellow Post-it notes; one had been torn off, and it had little doodles and words written on it.

I stared at the man intently and realised he looked familiar; oddly, he looked like Max.

I also found I wasn't the only spirit in the room: a stocky, Native American woman stood behind the left shoulder of the man at the table, and at his right stood a brawny suedehead wearing a green bomber jacket. A young boy dressed in a knight's costume peered from around his legs; he had the bluest eyes I'd ever seen.

I was mesmerised by the presence of the woman; she seemed to fill the entire room. She had long, black hair and jewellery made from colourful beads. Her eyes were closed, and she held her hands over the living man's head.

Tamara tapped her fingers on the table; she only did this out of nervousness and not impatience, which was a rare occurrence. She and the man were in deep conversation.

Knowing they probably couldn't hear me, I spoke to the spirits in the room.

'What's going on here?' I whispered.

'Shush, don't interrupt Thundering Mountain while she is talking to the universe,' said the man in the green jacket.

'What's a thundering mountain?' I asked, bewildered.

'Not a what,' he tutted. 'Thundering Mountain is David's spirit guide. She has summonsed you here. Wait and listen.'

I presumed the man at the table was David. The pair were silent as David looked at a card in his hand. The only sounds in the room were a ticking clock, crackling logs in the fireplace, and Tamara's fingers tapping away.

I inspected the rest of the room; to my right, a large fireplace looked out of place in the small room. In the centre stood a log burner. Ornate swords and candelabras decorated the hearth.

Out of the corner of my eye, I spotted a dark shadow in the opposite corner. As the figure emerged, I thought it looked like Eisen, but before his shape formed in its entirety, it disappeared.

David's voice broke the silence: 'This is your outcome card. The ship here indicates you will be doing a lot more travelling, both for work and holidays,' he said, showing Tamara the card.

'Wow, thank you. You've got many things spot on. I've always been wary and sceptical of people like you,' she said, her body slackening from its previously rigid position.

'You have every right to be. Many out there take advantage. I don't advertise my services; you've only found out about me through word of mouth. The money I receive for readings goes to charity.'

'That's truly kind of you.' Tamara smiled. 'I guess I should pay, then go.' But she started tapping the table again, showing no sign of leaving.

My mind clicked. Tamara had come for a reading from a psychic medium. I'd always thought she didn't believe in psychics and spirits.

'If you think you've heard all you came for…' David said, eyeing her over his glasses. 'But I think you came to ask me something specific. I don't think you wanted a reading at all.'

'Well, yes… How did you know?'

'Because I just told you, that's how,' he said flatly.

Tamara frowned. 'Fine. Is Caroline alright?'

'Why don't you ask your daughter?' He smiled.

Tamara pulled back in her seat and clutched her throat. 'H-how did you know?' she stammered.

'Because that's what you came to ask me in the first place.

You want to know if she really saw your friend.'

I gulped and waited for him to answer. This had to be why Thundering Mountain had summonsed me here.

'Well, did she?' Tamara edged forward in her seat.

I moved closer to hear his answer.

David leant back. 'I believe she did. Yes.'

Tamara recoiled. 'My god. I thought she made it all up, as though it was her way of dealing with Caroline's death. Is my daughter gifted like you?'

'Who knows?' he shrugged. 'Children are more susceptible to seeing spirits. She might grow out of it or develop further.'

'Okay...' Tamara said, looking down at the cards on the table. 'Is Caroline really alright?'

'Yes, I believe so. Though something looms heavy over her death.'

'What do you mean?'

Yes, what do you mean?

I edged even closer; I was almost at the table.

'The vision is cloudy, so I can't be sure. It's as though the accident was someone else's fault,' David replied.

'Well, yes, it was a car accident,' said Tamara.

'I'm not sure that's what I'm seeing. It's something else. I'm sorry, Tamara, it's not clear.'

Tamara nodded. She didn't look concerned by his revelation, but it sure had me rattled when I put it together with the other information that had been niggling away at me.

'All that aside, she has transitioned well, and she will be around if you need her. If you want to talk to her, just speak to her in your mind, and she will be close by. Just for future reference, if you see a robin or a white feather, that is usually a sign a loved one has popped by to say hello.'

CHAPTER TWELVE

'How do you know all these things?' asked Tamara.

'I've been given a gift, though I think we've all got it. People don't understand how easy it is to do.'

'If it's so easy, why aren't there more of you?'

'Everyone is capable. All they need to do is shut themselves off from media. Shut their eyes, shut out the noise, and believe more,' said David.

'That's easier said than done... I guess that's why my daughter has picked it up. Her television time is heavily restricted, and I don't allow her to play on any of my electronics.'

'That could be why, yes. I don't blame you for being sceptical. I used to be. I thought all mediums were fake. For me, everything had to have a reason for happening. I questioned everything around me.'

Tamara tilted her head. 'What changed?'

'Much like your daughter, something strange happened that I couldn't explain. I started having visions that came true. I realised a higher power had to be responsible, but I had no idea who or what it was. My spooky sister had always been into this sort of thing, whereas I pushed it all away.' He paused and rubbed his temples. 'My sister told me it was a person who had passed that was giving me these visions. I thought of people I knew in spirit and said their names in my mind until one name gave me a chill, so I knew who was with me.'

'Who was it?' asked Tamara.

'I can't tell you his name, but it was a little boy. His family didn't believe he had returned to watch over them,' he said and wiped beneath his glasses.

'That's so sad. Does it not freak you out? It certainly did me when my daughter first mentioned it.' She shuddered.

'A little to begin with; we are programmed to immediately

fear the unknown. And when I started, I wasn't sure what to believe, so I looked for answers, like you have today.' He started to collect the cards and put them in a box.

'How did you find answers? I want to understand in case my daughter starts asking me questions.'

'I went to a spiritual fair to have my own reading, but there were so many mediums to choose from, I ended up walking around the room three times.' He laughed. 'Then I looked at a woman who had a deck of Egyptian cards. She looked right at me and said the name Michael. I told her that wasn't my name, to which she replied, "No, but he's been with you a long time." I sat down when she said that. You see, I'd lost my best friend Michael years ago. The medium asked me how long I'd had the gift, and I told her on and off since childhood. She thought I had been this way for longer than I can remember.'

'What did you say to that? Did you believe her?' Tamara said. She put her elbow on the table and rested her chin on her hand.

'Not at the time. She put me in touch with a lady who conducted past life regressions. I don't know where all the memories came from, but they appeared to be mine.' He started to doodle on a blank Post-it note.

'That's wild.'

David laughed. 'Tell me about it. But finding out about spiritualism has really changed my whole outlook on life and how things work. I look deeply into everything, though I don't question it. It's my gift, and I can help others. I feel so much better within myself when I have.'

'Thank you, David. You really have given me a lot to think about.' Tamara stood up and held out her hand to shake David's.

CHAPTER TWELVE

He shook his head.

'I don't shake hands. I give hugs.' David stood up and hugged Tamara before she had a chance to protest. Her face turned red. Tamara had never been one for giving or receiving hugs, and I chuckled at her obvious discomfort.

I sat on the chair Tamara had vacated to take in all the information David had reeled off. He made some good points, but I doubted the mass population would be willing to give up social media to commune with their deceased loved ones.

The man in the green bomber jacket left David's side and approached me.

'I'm Mick,' he said.

I looked up. 'The Mick David mentioned?' I asked.

He smiled. 'The one and only.'

'And the little boy, is that him in the knight costume?' I pointed.

'Yep.'

'Man, can your friend talk a lot.'

'I know. He's not meant to do it for too long, but he's been known to chat to the same person for hours at a time.'

'I can believe it... So, you're not a spirit guide, are you?'

He shook his head. 'That's Thundering Mountain's job. I'm just at David's side whenever he needs me—which seems to be a lot lately,' he said, looking over my head, into the corner.

'You know Eisen, then,' he continued.

'Yes... How did you know that?' I said, eyeing him curiously.

'Well, you mentioned spirit guides, and he's behind you,' he said, indicating with his head.

'What?' I rose from the chair to find Eisen stood a few steps behind me, arms folded.

'What are you doing here?' I asked.

163

'Watching out for David,' he said.

'Really?' I asked. 'Or are you just following me?'

'Caroline, not everything is about you. At least not today, anyway,' he said, shaking his head.

'Not today?' I said.

Eisen ignored my question and walked past me to talk to Mick. I listened intently.

'How's he doing today, Mick?' Eisen asked.

'Not bad. No visits today.'

'Good,' said Eisen. 'Have you had chance to speak to Thundering Mountain about it?'

Mick nodded. 'She's not happy about you popping by, for starters.'

'I expected as much,' he said, looking over at her. She turned her head and avoided his gaze.

'She said he's getting stronger each time he visits, but there's nothing she can do, short of jumping in there herself and forcing him out, which she is reluctant to do.'

'Okay, I can appreciate that,' said Eisen.

'I'm sorry,' I interrupted, approaching the pair. I had no clue what they were going on about, and I was eager to learn more. 'But what's going on? Why all the secrecy?'

They both eyed me, then Mick shrugged.

'If you must know, Caroline, David is the man I told you about in the woods,' said Eisen.

I stared back at him blankly.

'Max's spirit keeps latching on to David.'

'Oh,' I said, remembering our conversation. 'So, this is him. That explains why he looks like him. Is he okay? He seems all right.'

'I don't see the resemblance, myself,' Eisen said, focusing on him. 'Right now, he is fine, but he's plagued by dreams and visions. He hides it well.'

'What does this have to do with me?' I asked.

'Nothing, and you said you didn't feel anything was different when I asked,' said Eisen flatly.

'Nothing? Then why am I here? And of course, I don't. I've nothing to compare it to, Eisen. I've only been here a short time!' I threw my arms up.

He shrugged. 'You being here is purely coincidental or the universe playing games.'

I rolled my eyes and stamped a foot, causing a glass of water on the table to ripple. 'Just for once, Eisen, I wish you could give me a straight, honest answer,' I said. 'It's like you're teetering on the edge of telling me something, then you change your mind.'

'All will be revealed,' he said.

'Stop saying that,' I snapped. 'If you can't be honest with me, then I'll be off.'

'Caroline, don't be like that.'

'Be like what? Oblivious to what's going around me? Blind to these supposed changes that are happening in the spirit world? If it has something to do with me, I'd rather know now instead of being kept dangling on a string. Now, if you don't mind, I'll be off.'

Eisen and Mick stepped back, obviously sensing my anger.

'Mick, Thundering Mountain, it was lovely to meet you both. Eisen, the next time you decide to drop by, I expect some answers.'

Chapter Thirteen

Numerous thoughts circled my mind.

Everyone I spoke to or overheard, seemed to imply that my death wasn't an accident. That something had been at work.

But who was responsible? James? Surely not. I couldn't contemplate it being him.

And what about the changes? Would they affect me? The lost souls or all of us?

I wanted a clear mind, to start over.

I needed to process all the information I had and work through it step by step until I could make sense of it all.

And I had only felt at peace with two people.

I went back to my parents and landed in their living room. The room looked the same as it had during my last visit, except for the shrine on the sideboard; all my pictures had been grouped together with candles and artificial flowers.

I scanned the room. All the pictures of my wedding had been removed. I wondered if my parents had found out about the affair.

I knew my dad hadn't been keen on my marriage to James; he thought I should date a few more men, since James had been my first long-term boyfriend. I reminded him he and my mother were high-school sweethearts and had only ever dated each other. It puzzled me how they could have found out, though. Perhaps I was reading too much into everything.

I heard voices in the kitchen and found my parents in there, dressed in their Sunday best and getting ready to leave. I wanted to spend time with them, so I snook out and got in the back of their car before they could see the door open and close.

My mother appeared first; she carried a medium-sized white box, tied with a purple ribbon. She opened the car door I sat nearest to, so I slid across to the middle seat. She placed the box down, pulled the seatbelt across, and buckled it in.

That's odd.

My father shuffled over the gravel drive and almost slipped. My mother yelled, 'Pick your feet up, Bob!' as she got in the passenger side of the car.

As my father joined her, he asked, 'Are you ready for this?'

'As ready as I can be, considering...' she replied.

'Okay. Let's go.'

I had no idea where they were going or what was so precious in the box to warrant it being strapped in. No matter the destination, spending time in the car with them reminded me of my childhood when we would go for day trips to the beach or the fair, then I'd fall asleep on the way home with my head on my mother's lap.

We hadn't travelled far when I noticed familiar scenery; my parents had taken the road to Saint Bees. I panicked. If they headed to the beach, I couldn't go with them.

I cursed myself for not thinking my actions through.

When we stopped, I'd have to get out of the car quickly to prevent drawing attention to myself.

I tried to make the most of the car journey. I laughed at my dad as he serenaded my mum by singing along to the radio. How I wished they could have heard me giggling away in the back seat.

They arrived at their destination and pulled into a carpark a short walk from the beach. When my mother retrieved the box from the back seat, I shot out through her, apologising profusely as she shivered.

I hung back to resist the pull of the beach as I followed. When I reached as far as I dared go, I stopped and watched them.

They interrupted their walk to change their shoes for sandals at a bench, then made a beeline for a group of people huddled together at the shore.

I edged a tiny bit forwards to get a better look. The group consisted of my friends: Dawn, Tamara, Raquel—I hadn't seen her at my funeral; no doubt she'd been travelling somewhere—and the last person in the group was Clare.

I had no clue why she'd come along to whatever this gathering was for. No doubt she'd be acting like a complete golden girl. My parents couldn't have known about the affair if she was here—unless they did know but were oblivious to who the affair had been with.

I shook my head. I felt as though I didn't know anything, anymore.

I couldn't risk going on the beach for fear of the invisible force that pulled spirits away, and I had to keep my distance from Clare, lest I lose control again.

My friends and Clare embraced my parents, then gathered in a circle. My mother placed the box she'd been carrying in the middle.

At this point, I moved forwards, curiosity getting the better of me. I wanted a better look at what was going on, but the group blocked my view.

They all held hands, then my mother bent over the box and undid the purple ribbon. The box released a flutter of butterflies: an array of blue, green, red, and orange wings swarmed around the group, then took off into the sky.

I now realised what I was witnessing; it was a memorial, and instead of releasing balloons, they had chosen to release butterflies in my honour—I could always count on my mother to protect the environment.

I could imagine Mum thinking I would be watching over them as the colours floated up towards me in the heavens.

It pissed me off Clare had been invited, though. No doubt she would have wormed her way in by spouting on about representing the company or something. What a two-faced bitch she had shown herself to be, and now she was giving a speech. *The nerve.*

I wanted to hear what she was saying, and so I crept closer. Just as I reached a bench that abutted the sand, something powerful grabbed at me from all angles, yanking me several steps forward in the space of a heartbeat.

I screamed, struggling to find my footing on the sand to no avail. It was just as Daniel had described—like a giant magnet forcing me across the beach.

I fought back with everything I had when two hands grabbed me around the waist and yanked me to safety.

We landed in a tangled heap on the footpath, and I scrambled away from the arms that held me close. I glanced over my shoulder; my rescuer was Daniel.

'What are you doing here?' I exclaimed, jumping away from him to almost collide with a group of cyclists.

'I could ask you the same thing. Didn't I tell you not to get too close to the sea?' he said, brushing himself off as he stood—though I hardly saw the point, as no sand clung to us.

'Yes, but I wasn't even that close. I didn't even put one foot on the beach. Until...until whatever that was.' I shook my head in disbelief.

'Doesn't matter. The distance to the sea is shorter here compared to where we first met.'

I clenched my jaw. 'Right. Well, I need to go now,' I said.

'Are you forgetting something?' he asked.

'No, I don't think I am. I need to be in a place where you aren't,' I blurted, but instantly regretted my words as I watched his face droop.

'A *thank you* would have been nice...' he grunted quietly. 'And it would also be nice to know why you keep running away from me.'

'Um, thank you... and I didn't mean to say that,' I said, avoiding the sad look on his face.

'You obviously did, otherwise you wouldn't have said it,' he retorted.

I sighed. I guessed I may as well tell him what Jane told me; then he might stop popping up when I least expected it. Though I was thankful he had shown up today.

'Jane told me you're dangerous,' I said, stepping away.

'What?' he scoffed, then laughed. 'And you believe her?'

I shrugged.

'Let me guess, she told you I almost scared someone to death.'

'Yes, she did, actually. And I saw you over that woman the other day. What was that about?' I asked.

'What a load of chicken shittery,' he said, rubbing the back of his neck.

CHAPTER THIRTEEN

'You didn't answer me,' I said, watching him as he started to pace.

'Take what Jane says with a pinch of salt. It was her who scared someone to the brink of death. And the woman you saw the other day, she fell off her bike; I hung around until someone helped her. You must see that Caroline.' His eyes pleaded with me. 'I've only ever shown up to help you.'

I looked down, embarrassed for believing her. Of course, he had only ever tried to assist me. What an idiot I'd been.

'Perhaps I should have chosen my friends more wisely,' I muttered.

'Pardon?'

'Nothing.' Then I groaned loudly, crouched down, and put my head between my legs. 'Why is this life so hard?'

'It doesn't have to be,' said Daniel, sitting in front of me.

I lowered my bum to the floor and crossed my legs.

'Are we staying in the middle of this path, then?' he raised an eyebrow.

'Sure. Not many people about, is there?'

Daniel's eyes swept the area. 'Guess not.' He shrugged.

'So, what did you do to Jane? I mean, you must have done something to make her say those things about you.' I looked into his face; he was handsome in a rugged way. I averted my eyes quickly, thankful I no longer blushed.

'Well,' he puffed his cheeks out, 'she started changing... and disappearing for long periods of time. I eventually tracked her down with her friends and caught them in the act of playing havoc in someone's house.'

I tutted, then recalled what I'd almost done in Clare's house.

'I threatened to tell Frankie G,' he continued. 'She didn't like that, and there were six of them and only one of me. We broke up, and the rest is history, as they say. I've been at the beach ever since. Some people from the pub come and see me, but I've never disclosed why I've not been back.'

'I'm sorry I believed her... and for acting like an arse.'

He laughed, and his electric-blue eyes sparkled.

How had I not noticed them before?

'It's my fault, Caroline,' he said, bringing a hand to his chest. 'I shouldn't have sent you there in the first place. I ought to have known better.' He looked down, letting his hair fall over his cheeks.

'It's not your fault, Daniel. I have my own mind, and I went along with them.' I looked into his eyes; they were mesmerising.

'I'm glad I found you today. I've been searching for you all over the place, and whenever I did find you, you ran off.' He smirked.

'Sorry about that...' I said, returning his smile.

Daniel crossed his legs and shuffled closer to me. I gulped, until now I hadn't really looked at Daniel except to figure out if he was crazy or not. Now my eyes were truly open to him.

Could he be the person who was meant to join me on my path?

'Can I ask what you're doing here? This was the last place I expected to find you, but I took a chance in the hope you might feel the need to see me.'

'Well, sorry to burst your bubble, but see those folks down there?' I pointed. 'Those are my parents and some of my friends; they're holding a memorial for me here, and I'm just watching.'

He laughed. 'Okay, that's nice. But haven't you got anything better to do?'

'Probably.' I shrugged, then pulled my hands into my lap as a seagull pecked in a circle to my right.

'Then why aren't you doing it?' he asked, his eyes gleaming. Then he smiled a toothy grin.

'Why are you smiling at me like that?' I asked, but my mouth tugged upwards; his smile was infectious. And his eyes, well, I could just melt into them.

'You're cute when you're angry,' he said out of nowhere.

'You haven't seen me angry,' I scoffed and folded my arms.

He leant forward, and I caught a slight whiff of musk and cedarwood.

'What are you doing?' I rubbed my hands over my face. 'Is there something on my face?'

He laughed heavily, making his shoulders shake.

'What?' I huffed not just him but at the seagull now squawking at a man walking past with a sandwich.

'Caroline, you can't get something on your face,' he said, tilting his head.

'Oh, hah. I forgot. Then why are you invading my personal space?'

'I want to ask you out, or whatever the kids call it these days,' he said.

'You and me?' I spluttered, pointing at the both of us. I *definitely* hadn't seen that coming.

'I want to take you out. I've not stopped thinking about you since the first time I saw you. You've driven me wild chasing after you,' he sighed.

My stomach fluttered. 'Really? Why?'

'Your enthusiasm when I first met you. You drove me crazy with your questions. Since you left, your smile has been engrained in my mind. I've hoped and prayed I'd find you and get the chance to speak to you properly.' He winked.

I looked into his eyes again; they shined with desire for me. I'd never seen a look like that in any man, not even James. I melted at his words, his eyes, and his scent.

He got up and held out his hands to help me up.

My legs resembled two lumps of lead as he took my hand and led me to a nearby bench. We walked around the seagull and its newly arrived friend.

'So, will you?' he coaxed, bringing a hand to my face to stroke my cheek.

I know it's not possible, but it was as though all the air had been sucked from my lungs. I pressed my cheek further into his palm and savoured his soft touch.

'Wow,' I mumbled.

He let out a soft growl and gazed into my eyes, eagerly waiting for my answer.

'Well... I... I mean,' I stumbled over the right words to say.

'I'm taking that as a yes,' he said.

'I never expected this to happen when I set out this morning,' I said. Especially as I previously thought him a kook for all his wild beliefs—maybe Jane had driven him mad.

'Neither did I. To be honest, I don't know what came over me. I've never been so forward before. I've not been myself since I first saw you, and every time since, I've regretted suggesting you go to that damn pub,' he hissed.

I took his hand from my cheek and held it in mine. 'Daniel, don't blame yourself. There's every chance I would have ended up there, anyway. It's not your fault.'

'Thank you for saying that and for believing in me. Jane was a complete nightmare. I'd hoped when I sent you off there that you'd be introduced to the nice ones. Sadly, she appears to

CHAPTER THIRTEEN

have weaved a web of magic around Frankie G; he's oblivious to the goings on.'

'Well, no damage done except to my pride,' I laughed.

'Best to put it all behind us. What do you say?' he asked.

'I agree. So, what now?'

'Right now, heads up and listen,' he said, looking past me.

'To... what?'

'Bunch of schoolchildren coming. Chances are one might be able to see us.'

'Oh,' I said, my eyes wide.

I listened for the sounds of the kids; their high-pitched laughs carried on the breeze. I could hear two or three of them yelling '*Miss, Miss,*' at their teacher.

We both glanced towards them as their footsteps got nearer. They were almost identical in their red and black uniforms. They all carried blue rucksacks. '*Miss, Miss,*' some continued to yell out.

'What's all this *Miss* business?' a woman said at the front of the group. She had reddish-orange hair and wore a perfectly fitted tweed jacket. 'Just call me Celeste,' she said.

The group passed without any of the children spotting us.

'Phew,' Daniel puffed his cheeks out. 'Now it's time for our first date,' Daniel said standing and pulling me to my feet.

'Now?' I asked.

'Yes, now. We've got better things to do.'

I laughed. 'Have we now?'

'Yep, so where to?'

'Um...' I needed a moment to think. Even though I was attracted to Daniel, people in the pub clearly thought he was nuts.

'What? You can tell me anything, Caroline. I'd rather you

were upfront with me. I had enough lies with Jane.'

'Okay, well, what it is… When we first met…well, I thought you were a bit bonkers with your conspiracy theories. And then when I went to the pub, they laughed at the mention of your name and asked what theory you were on about this week.'

Daniel laughed. 'Caroline, you don't have to believe my "theories,"' he said, using air quotes. 'People can believe in different things and still get along. And it doesn't mean they're crazy. But if you would like, I'd be happy to tell you more.'

I grinned. 'Sure, I'd love to hear what you have to say.'

'Excellent, let's go.'

'Wait, I want to say goodbye to my friends and parents first,' I said, glancing back at the group.

'Okay, sure, I'll take you as far as I think is safe.'

'Thank you, Daniel.'

We walked back towards the beach; the group were now sat on picnic blankets, eating and drinking out of paper cups.

'Goodbye!' I yelled. 'Love you all, see you next week!'

'You might not be here next week,' Daniel remarked.

I frowned. 'What do you mean?'

'I might have whisked you away to a faraway land.' He pointed out towards the sea, and I giggled like a lovestruck teenager; no one had ever offered to whisk me away anywhere.

'We can come back for a visit though, can't we? I promised my gran I'd visit all my loved ones once a week,' I told him.

'Whatever it takes to keep that smile on your face.' He grinned at me. 'Where would you like to go first?'

Thinking on my feet, I suggested the Natural History Museum. I didn't want to leave the country just yet.

CHAPTER THIRTEEN

* * *

I barely took in the exhibits as we walked around the museum; everything was a blur to me. All I could focus on was Daniel as he told me about his death and a bit more about Jane. I wouldn't normally want to know the ins and outs of a potential partner's dating history, but seeing as I knew her, I had to know all the details. I couldn't start our relationship without full disclosure.

The end of his relationship with Jane had driven him to the beach, and he never left until he met me. The home he had lived in got knocked down and turned into flats. He had visited it, but the sense of it being his home had vanished, and the beach became his new home.

We talked and walked around the entire museum, though I couldn't remember what I'd seen except for the blue whale and dinosaur bones in the main hall. I explained to him how I had come to want to take revenge on Clare, and he agreed to help me, should we ever bump into her again. He also told me he wanted to spend as much time with me as possible, and I couldn't say no.

He filled me in on the world's conspiracy theories that he had gathered from his father's research—such as Paul McCartney being dead (which made me laugh out loud), the CIA creating AIDS, and all major heads of state were really reptilian humanoids sent to enslave the human race. He spoke with such intelligence and passion, it was hard to disagree with the points he raised.

Now, I didn't believe half of what he told me; they were like fairy tales for adults, if you asked me. But we spend the majority of our childhoods believing in Santa and the tooth fairy without any proof; I wasn't going to let a few stories get in the way of my future happiness.

Those few initial hours we spent together told me he had to be the person Eisen said I should spend my time with. I was positive he was my destiny on this spiritual plane.

I took him to my home, and there we stayed for days as we shared our pasts and learnt each other's dreams.

We shared our first kiss, which was hot and heavy, and despite being unable to do more due to the problem that spirits can't remove their clothes, our relationship blossomed quickly, and I forgot all about why I had gone to my parents' house. All my problems and niggles fluttered away as I enjoyed his company.

I had nine years and eleven months left to enjoy the world with Daniel, and my worries were far behind me.

Chapter Fourteen

Two months had passed since the day on the beach, and Daniel and I had become inseparable.

And though I hadn't seen her since my funeral, I'd kept the promise I made to my grandmother and visited everyone weekly, no matter where we were in the world. Daniel came with me on every visit, too. He said with each one, he felt like he knew them a little better.

We had arrived back in the UK two days earlier and were spending our time visiting all the places in York which claimed to be haunted. We hadn't met a single spirit so far, and Daniel had become annoyed with all the false advertisements. I changed the subject to ease his disappointment, and so we could discuss some of his theories further. I really wanted to understand what made him tick.

'It's a load of old poppycock, all these conspiracy theories,' I said as we walked down The Shambles. We'd passed a book shop claiming to sell a book on every conspiracy theory under the sun, but I'd refused to go in.

'Poppycock? What are you, ninety? You sound like my gran,' he joked.

I tutted. 'You know what I mean.'

'Well, I know it's not *poppycock*. My uncle's friend's cousin's friend knew somebody who worked on the Roswell Incident, and it was in my dad's research,' he said, puffing his chest out.

'What? Your uncle's… friend's… cousin's… friend?' I laughed, clutching my sides 'You've got to be kidding me. I'll catch my pants, at this rate!'

'No, I'm serious, Caroline. It's true.'

'*Okay*, Daniel.'

He shook his head and stopped outside a sweetshop that claimed to have a ghost. 'You just don't understand,' he mumbled.

I paused and looked at the old-fashioned sweets lined up in jars along the back wall. He was right, I didn't. At least, not without any concrete evidence.

'Right, then, let's go,' I said.

'What, in there?' He pointed to the shop.

'No—to Area 51.'

'What?' He snorted. 'No.'

'Come on, what are you waiting for? We'll go look right now and find out the truth.'

Daniel stared wide-eyed at me.

'Daniel, you believe in this wholeheartedly without any proof. Don't you think it's about time you got some?'

'Well, I have considered going many times, but I've felt too uncomfortable to go on my own.'

'Uncomfortable? Like when you were little and you daren't go to the toilet in case you needed help to wipe your arse?' I laughed again. Anyone who could hear us would think we hated each other, the way I ribbed him.

'No,' he said and walked into the shop, keeping his back to me. 'I don't know why I bother telling you half the time.'

'Come on, don't be off with me. You love the banter as much

CHAPTER FOURTEEN

as I do.'

He turned and smiled. 'I know, babe. So, which is your favourite sweet?'

'Pear drops. Now, don't change the subject. Do you want to go or not? I'll not offer to go again.'

He grinned that toothy grin I loved so much. 'I want to go look.'

'Good. Do you know where to head for? Or do we need to bang our heels together three times to get across the pond?'

'Just take my hand. We're going to Nevada, not Kansas,' he laughed.

I grabbed his hand, and in a flash, we'd arrived in a vast, dimly lit warehouse with a fusty smell. It took a minute for my eyes to adjust.

'Where are we?' I asked him.

'A hangar in Area 51.'

'Is there more than one?'

He shrugged. 'I dunno, my father only mentioned this one.'

I looked around. Nothing shouted out to me that it might contain extra-terrestrial artefacts. A few dozen wooden crates had been dumped in a corner, and a single fighter jet stood in the middle.

'Where's the UFO, Daniel? There's only a fighter jet, albeit a strange-shaped one,' I said, eyeing the nose of the thing.

He reached up and rubbed its fuselage, then walked around it. 'It's a stealth fighter jet,' he said as he continued to inspect it. 'Look at the dark colour, and there's no country of origin marked on it that I can see.'

I hummed, already growing bored. 'I think we should keep looking around, don't you?'

I spotted a door illuminated by an emergency light and

propped open by a fire extinguisher. I headed over to it, and Daniel followed.

The door led to a thin corridor and a flight of stairs going downwards.

'Look, cameras.' I pointed and waved to the blinking red eye in the corner as we descended the stairs.

'Stop that,' Daniel hissed.

'What's wrong? They can't see us.'

'I just don't think we should be messing around in a military installation.'

'Ooh, get you. *Military installation*. There's no one here.'

We continued to climb down the flights, and I resisted the desire to dance the macarena in front of every security camera. However, after the fifth flight, the novelty grew thin.

'How far does this place go down?' I whined.

Daniel looked over the bannister. 'I think a couple more flights, but let's stop here if you want and look around.'

As we searched the floor, we found a locker room and a room with several rifle racks. Daniel convinced himself of their importance.

'If there is nothing here to protect, why do they need rifles, aye?'

I shrugged. 'I have no idea. Because it's America—something to do with the fifth amendment.'

'I think you mean the second amendment.'

'Yeah, and that one.' A light flickered over my head, and the bulb popped, making me squeal. Daniel promptly shushed me.

'Is that someone coming?' I asked, my hand on my chest.

'No, I don't think so. It was just the light.'

'God, you would think I wouldn't get spooked anymore, but it's worse than ever.'

CHAPTER FOURTEEN

'It's not every day you get to creep around a secret base, is it? Even if we are dead,' he said, browsing the lockers.

'Have you even looked at these rifles?' I said, inspecting the thick layer of dust. 'They haven't been touched in years.'

'There's got to be something here worth seeing,' he said, turning a full 360 degrees to scan the room.

'Look, Daniel, you don't need to prove anything to me. If you say there are aliens and spaceships, then I believe you.'

Daniel sighed. 'One more room, then we'll go. There's got to be an autopsy room somewhere.'

I trailed behind, guilt-ridden for suggesting the visit and for Daniel's mounting disillusion.

I followed him into another room full of aluminium screens. Rubber sheets had been placed between them, as if to stop people peering through the gaps. We weaved through them and discovered an operating theatre with lights and utensils, untouched for years just like the rifles.

'Look, I told you! I knew I was right.' Daniel pointed to the table, practically dancing on his toes.

'It's more likely a sick bay for whoever used to work here.' I glanced around. 'Look, here's a huge first-aid box. Babe, I'm sorry, but you can't piece together what isn't there.'

'Well, what's that, then?'

I followed his finger and noticed a door at the end of the room. As we approached, I spotted a panel next to it; it looked like it required a palm print.

'We will never get in there.'

'Shh, let me think,' said Daniel as he paced up and down.

I folded my arms. 'Fine.'

'I've got it!' he shouted. 'If you think about it, the print is already on the scanner.'

'And?' I coaxed.

'And if I apply pressure to it, it should scan what's already been there.'

I rolled my eyes. 'If you say so.'

'Okay, here it goes.' He placed his palm on the scanner and pressed down hard. A red beam passed under his hand, then beeped. 'It worked!' he yelled.

'Oh yeah, if it worked, why hasn't the door opened, *Daniel*?'

'Umm…'

Another laser appeared above our heads. It scanned the whole room, first lengthways, then sideways. Then an ear-splitting alarm pierced the air.

'What the hell!'

'What have you done?' I yelled over the noise.

'Get in that corner.'

I ignored his instruction and followed him into his corner 'I'm staying with you,' I said and wrapped my arms around him.

'Okay, but stay still.'

The door we'd tried to access flung open, and in ran two armed guards dressed in black. One of their radio's crackled, then came to life.

'Status update, over,' said a voice with a thick American drawl.

'In Grey's entrance, all looks secure. Must be a glitch again. They oughta be updating the system. It's from the darn nineties, Hank. Over.'

'Grey's entrance,' whispered Daniel. 'That's got to be the way to the alien stuff. They are always referred to as Greys.'

'No, no, no.' I pulled away a little to look at him. 'There is no way I'm going further. We've already triggered the alarms!'

CHAPTER FOURTEEN

I exclaimed.

The guards gave the room another once over, then asked for it to be rescanned. The lasers reappeared and set the alarms off again, this time accompanied by a computer-generated voice.

'Foreign entities identified. Initiating lockdown. Stand clear of all doors in three seconds. Three...'

I pulled Daniel closer to me. 'They're picking up our presence, Daniel.'

'Two...' counted down the robot voice.

Daniel gulped. 'Yeah. I think that's our cue to leave.'

He took us out of the room, and we landed in the middle of a road. I figured the experience had rattled him. We had never landed in a random area before. Three bikes and their riders passed through us before Daniel got his act together. Each rider glanced over their shoulder, no doubt perplexed by the sudden drop in temperature. We dashed to the pavement to avoid any other vehicles passing through us.

'Where have you taken us?' I asked.

'Scarborough,' he said calmly, as though the last five minutes hadn't happened. 'Awesome—there's a few scooters here today!' he said his eyes focused on the rows of scooters painted in every colour of the rainbow, lined up along the seafront.

'Aren't we going to talk about what just happened?'

'There's nothing to talk about.' He headed off without me.

I threw my arms up. I couldn't fathom his reason for dismissing the danger we had faced. Some unknown government agency had machines that could detect spirits!

'There *is* something to talk about,' I said as I reached his side.

'Nope, we didn't see anything. End of,' he said, still admiring the scooters.

'Daniel, how can you be so blasé about it? We were almost

discovered by some government agency. Even though the people couldn't see us, their machines still caught us. Don't you think we should tell someone?'

'Don't be daft, we were never in any danger, and who would we tell? I'll always take care of you, and we got out safely, didn't we?'

I nodded. 'But—'

He turned to face me. 'Sweetheart, they just had a dicky system, that's all. Do you really think there's a machine out there that can detect us?' he said, rubbing my arms.

'I don't know.' I paused to think. 'Probably not. But still, why did they have that kind of security in the first place if there's nothing there?'

'I dunno, and I don't care to talk about it anymore,' he said flatly.

'Fine.'

'Good. Now, can we go look at the scooters?'

I let the topic drop and followed like a mardy teenager cajoled into a family day out. Daniel *oohed* and *aahed* over the scooters. They were painted with fancy murals and adorned with different embellishments. He told me the name for each one, but they all flew over my head. The only two wheels I'd been on was a pushbike.

He spent ages over a swanky green scooter, which he told me was not any old green but candy-apple green. And he laughed when I told him they all looked the same to me.

While he bent to check out the white-walled tyres, I heard a woman shout. I looked up to see a woman with long, wavy, blonde hair stood in a little doorway across the road. She reminded me of the pin-up girls from the forties and fifties.

Her eyes were focused on me, and she spoke through gritted

CHAPTER FOURTEEN

teeth: 'Come over here, now!'

'Daniel?'

His head popped up from behind a bike. 'Yeah?'

'We need to go. We're wanted over there.' I pointed.

'Who is it?' he asked.

'I don't know. Some woman. I think she's a spirit like us.'

'But I haven't looked at them all yet,' he whined.

I dragged Daniel over before he had the chance to look at another one.

'It's nice to meet another spirit.' I held out my hand to shake hers.

'Don't touch me.' She shivered. 'It gives me the heebie-jeebies. I'm not a spirit.'

I snatched my hand back. 'Sorry, my mistake.'

Daniel tutted. *'Caroline.'*

'Come on inside, only I can see you, and I don't want people seeing me talking to myself again. Folks already think I'm nuts,' she said.

Daniel and I gave each other a bemused glance and stepped through the door into a darkened room; a round table filled the centre and on it sat a crystal ball. Red velvet curtains were draped all over. An older gentleman sat in a corner; he wore a suit with medals pinned on it. I thought he had to be her spirit guide, though she didn't acknowledge his presence.

The woman sat at the table. 'I'm Theresa, the local fortune teller.'

'Bit late, aren't you love?' said Daniel. 'We're already dead.'

I stifled a laugh.

'I know that, clever clogs. You were both far too young to have passed. You seem a genuinely nice couple, though.'

'We aren't an "official couple,"' I air-quoted. 'I'm married to someone still living, I think.' I had no idea if James was alive.

'That's not what I see. You are incredibly lucky to have found each other on the other side. It's rare to get a second chance at love.' She smiled warmly.

Daniel leaned over and kissed me on the cheek. 'I am lucky, I suppose,' he said.

I warm sensation spread over me. Daniel hadn't told me he loved me yet, but I could tell he did.

'Caroline, you felt a warm sensation then, didn't you? I can feel the love cocooning the two of you.'

I raised my eyebrows. 'Wow, you're good.'

'I feel you have been betrayed in a past relationship,' she said, focusing on me.

'Yes.' I looked down at my feet. 'Haven't most people?'

'No, not everyone, Caroline. Just because you have been hurt doesn't mean you have to be cynical. You were just too trustworthy and kind to notice. All the signs were there.'

'I did mention some things to my friends. They dismissed it, though,' I told her.

'Don't you have anything to say about me?' Daniel chimed in.

'You died in an accident that wasn't your fault,' said Theresa.

'So did Caroline. I'm going to need more confirmation.'

'A car pulled out on you at a junction.'

'Yeah, it did.' Daniel took hold of my hand and squeezed. 'I saw them coming, too. I just didn't have the time to swerve.' His drop in tone made me squeeze back.

'Caroline, someone caused your accident; they did something to your car.'

I dropped Daniel's hand. 'What?'

She turned away. 'That's all I can tell you. I've said too much

CHAPTER FOURTEEN

already. You should leave.'

'What!'

The table shook, and the drapes fluttered.

'Caroline, calm down. We've been asked to leave. Let's go,' Daniel urged.

But I moved from his side, farther into the room. 'No, I'm not leaving! She can't tell me half a story, then ask me to leave.'

'You really should leave,' said Theresa. She stood and caught the crystal ball as it fell off its stand. 'I've got other customers to see, and I don't want my precious items breaking.'

'I'm not a customer. You called us over,' I spat. 'We didn't seek you out!'

Theresa opened the door, and a young woman entered. At the same time, Daniel darted across to me and ushered me out.

'Ooh, it's cold in here…' The woman rubbed her arms.

Theresa fixed me with an icy stare where I stood on the doorstep. 'Just the breeze when I opened the door. It will soon warm back up.'

I stared at the door after Theresa closed it in my face. She had dumped this news at my feet and expected me to take it and run.

'Daniel, we can't leave. I need to go back in there. I need to know what happened,' I rambled.

'She can only tell you what she knows. If she knew more, she would have told you.'

'But what about the police officer who spoke to my dad about my car? She has to know more about that, surely. And others have hinted at more, but I pushed it all away after we met again at the beach. Now it's all flooding back!' I exclaimed, pulling at my hair.

Daniel shook his head. 'Caroline, listen to me; she will have told you everything she can. What's done is done.'

I groaned. 'I need to know more, Daniel. I can't carry on with my time here knowing somebody intentionally hurt me. I want to know who did it and why!'

'What if it was James, aye? What then? How is that going to make you feel?' he said, taking me in his arms.

'I don't know...' I spoke into his chest. 'I don't have all the answers right now.'

'And if you found out who did it, what would you do? You can't talk to them.'

'Thanks for being so supportive...' I mumbled.

Daniel sighed. 'Is this really important to you, Caroline?'

'Yes, I really need to know. I can feel it gnawing away in the pit of my stomach. It's going to drive me insane not knowing the truth.'

Daniel's shoulders slumped forwards, his arms hanging limp at his sides. 'If you feel that way, you need to leave and find a way to access the truth. If you don't, it will torment you, and you'll be left here in limbo, regardless of the time you have been allocated.'

I glanced up at him and saw the desperation in his eyes. 'Daniel, what does that mean?'

'Now you know you died by the hand of another, it will eat away at you until eventually you turn into a reoccurring spirit. I couldn't bear to lose you to that hell...' he trailed off.

'A reoccurring spirit?'

'Your memories will consume you as you try to piece together what happened. You will be forced to replay your last living day, hours, or minutes over and over again.'

'You mean a lost soul? I met one in London—rather, she pushed me out of her path.' I began to pace the pavement. 'I

CHAPTER FOURTEEN

can't be like her. Daniel, you've got to help me,' I said as the horrifying face that emerged from the fog flashed through my mind.

'I'm sorry, I can't. This isn't like when I saved you on the beach,' he said.

I clasped my hands together and pleaded. 'Daniel, I need your help. You keep me grounded. I'm better when I'm with you.'

'I wish I could help, believe me,' he said, placing a hand over his heart. 'It's not my passing. This is something you need to do on your own.' He averted his gaze. 'I'm going back to where we met, and I'll wait for you there.'

'Daniel?' I cried.

He reached into his pocket and pulled out a Saint Christopher on a pendant. 'Put this in your bag. It will keep you safe. And be quick, Caroline, you don't have much time.'

'But—'

He vanished.

Chapter Fifteen

Once I returned home, everything came flooding back.

The memories from my final day. Our lives. The lies and betrayal.

The snippets of information I'd pushed away.

I prowled the house, looking for clues, to answer the questions whirling around in my head.

All my clothes and possessions had gone, as had the pictures with me in them.

I searched James's office for any signs that he may have had a part in my death. I rifled through paperwork and files; nothing shouted out to me. I expected to see a huge life insurance policy taken out in my name or some secret bank account, but there was nothing like that.

I couldn't even find anything that linked him to Clare; all I could think about is why he hadn't braked.

Deflated, I sat in the kitchen and replayed the memory of the day I died. I had to dig deep and push away the gnawing in the pit of my stomach.

The memories replayed in my head like an old-fashioned movie reel. We'd had breakfast, I'd checked the calendar on the fridge and reminded James that his car had been booked into the garage for its MOT that morning.

James slammed his mug on the breakfast bar, sloshing coffee onto the granite. 'Shit,' he uttered.

'Don't worry, I'll clean it up,' I said, grabbing the kitchen roll.

'Not that; I've got meetings all over this morning. Can I take your car?'

'That's fine, I'll follow you down, and you can drop me home. I'll ride in.'

'Are you sure?'

'Of course, babe. I like the ride in.'

'You're a star. What would I do without you?' he said, then kissed me on the head while I soaked up the spilt coffee. He tapped his watch. 'Five minutes, then I need to go.'

'Okay, let me change my shoes.'

I followed James to the garage, then he drove me home where I collected my bike.

I recalled the events at work. I'd presented the plan for the week ahead to the team, collected James's suits from the dry cleaner, had lunch, got the semi-promotion—although, now I think that was just a ploy to get me out of the way so Clare could spend more time with James.

Nothing out of the ordinary had occurred. It had been like any other Monday, the day I used to detest. I'd chosen to no longer hate the day; Daniel had made me see I had nothing to fear of Mondays. He would make a point of always taking us to a new place on the day.

I suddenly remembered James had texted me on my way back to the office at lunchtime, so I checked my ghost phone, and for some unknown reason, I could still retrieve his messages.

'Car passed MOT, but the brakes on your car seem dodgy. I'll book it into the garage for a check in a couple of days. Xoxo.'

I'd forgotten about the message. How could I forget that? Surely, I would have questioned it, wouldn't I? Or maybe not. I had been excited about the prospects of my promotion. Plus, the car seemed fine the day before, I think. I'd had no issues with the brakes on the way to the garage, either, albeit it was only a five-minute drive away.

The only thing I could think to do next was check at the police station and see how their investigation had panned out. I knew it wouldn't be easy, but I had to try.

I focused on the local police station and landed in a bustling room. I guess you would call it an incident room. There were three men and two women in the room, some in standard-issue uniforms, others in suits. Phones were ringing, and I could smell burnt coffee and pastries.

I didn't know where to start, I had no clue how a police station ran, where their files on me would be kept. Was it all carried out online? Or did they have paper files?

I decided to work my way from the back of the room inwards. I walked round the desks to the back; there I found the source of the smells I'd encountered. The coffee pot looked in need of a good scrub, and there were two croissants and two cinnamon whirls on a china plate.

Two suited men sat at this end—probably the ones who loved the coffee and pastries.

I peered over the first man's shoulder; he was a heavy smoker from the whiff that came off his clothes and his yellow-stained fingers. He was typing away on some sort of database on his laptop, and he had several files on the edge of his desk. The first one had a sticker with a name on, which was a good start. I gently nudged it to reveal the file underneath, not my name, I tried again and accidentally knocked the top file onto the

CHAPTER FIFTEEN

floor.

'What the?' the officer uttered as the file fell. 'Who's turned on the damn air con again?' he said to the room. All he got in response were blank faces.

I quickly stepped back as he bent to retrieve it. It hadn't revealed my name, so I moved on to the next desk. This also proved fruitless.

The next bank of desks seated the two female officers. I repeated the process with their files, and with the second woman, I hit the jackpot. There was a file with my name on, and I could see the corner of an orange Post-it note slapped on top of it. I couldn't move the file above mine without raising suspicion, and there was no way I'd be able to read it.

I either had to wait for her to leave her desk or create a distraction to force her to get up. When I thought about it, a distraction was out of the question; there were too many people. If I knocked something over, who knows who would get out of their seat to investigate.

I snooped round the rest of the room while I waited. There was nothing really of interest to look at. A few minutes passed when someone knocked at the door; a young blond guy popped his head round.

'Giles, Peters, King, boss wants to see you; room five,' he said, then quickly closed the door.

The two women and the bloke nearest the coffee machine got up and left, leaving me alone with just two remaining witnesses. I sat at the now vacated desk and slowly moved the file covering mine. There were in fact two Post-it notes on my file. They looked to be fresh, as they hadn't curled up or come unstuck.

The first one read '*ICE not wife!!!*' and the second read '*Brakes*

195

loosened, possibly leaked out over twenty-four hours depending on usage and force.'

'What the hell!' I shouted. The lights above my head flickered, and a few loose papers rustled.

'What was that?' one of the officers asked.

'Dunno. Power surge, probably,' answered the other.

How dare James change his *in case of emergency* to that bitch. And who had tampered with the brakes on my car? There was only one person who could possibly know the answer: James.

I clenched my fists, and the lights flickered again. I tore out of the police station and arrived at the hospital. The lights continued to flash above my head, and the overbed trolley wobbled. I relaxed my fists, and the room stilled.

James had been moved to another side room; everything was the same, except it was the opposite way round.

Monday morning have breakfast, check the calendar on the fridge.

It had started. Upon seeing his face, my memories now threatened to spill out, and I had to fight hard to resist an unseen power that tried to force me back home.

James still appeared to be in a coma. The bandages had been removed, and his bruised eye was nothing but a yellow smudge. He'd always been a slow healer and bruised easily; I'd lost count of how many times he'd come home from squash with bruises bigger than plates on his thighs.

James your car is booked in for its MOT today.

Another memory slipped out as I stood in the corner to avoid any visitors. I don't know how long I'd stood there before the door opened, and his parents walked in.

His mother, Joan, dashed straight to his side; his father, Charles, lingered behind. James was an only child like me. His mother had treated him like a prince, and he'd been fortunate to have a public-school education, thanks to his father's connections.

Clean the spilled coffee.

'He's looking better today, don't you think so, Charles?' said his mother as she swept his hair back.

I'm cycling to work today.

'He looks the same as yesterday and the day before.'

'No, his skin looks brighter today—less grey,' she said cheerfully.

'Joan, he never looked grey in the first place; he wasn't malnourished,' he said and cracked his knuckles. That used to infuriate me; it was worse than nails on a chalkboard for me.

She snorted. 'That's debatable.'

'Charming, Joan,' I muttered. 'As if I would starve your precious little lamb.'

'Let's focus on getting him better and out of this coma. Doesn't matter what he looks like.' Charles paced up and down. 'I want him awake. It's been three months, for pity's sake.'

Damn it, I've got soaked in the rain.

'Sit down, Charles. You're making me dizzy.'

'You know I can't stand this place. I'm not sitting down.'

Joan sniffed. 'Fine. What are we going to tell him about Caroline?'

This should be good, I thought.

Charles threw his arms up and then slapped his thighs. 'The truth, god damn it,' he said through gritted teeth. 'Do we have to go through this on a daily basis? The doctor said if he remembers the accident, then to tell him straight away. It's something to do with starting the healing process.'

Monday morning, give the presentation at work. Stupid Sophia.

I liked Joan and Charles. Yes, they could bicker like you wouldn't believe, and yes, we'd had our differences—mainly my reluctance to continue working and not start a family straight away. I'd had to remind them on more than one occasion that I had been brought up to work and would continue to do so no matter what. We hadn't told them we'd been trying to get pregnant; it was supposed to be a surprise.

But when all was said and done, they were good people, and I didn't envy them one bit when it came to supporting James through the next stages of his life, despite the pain he had caused me.

'My beautiful, caring boy,' Joan whispered over and over.

I snorted. *You won't have the same view after you find out he's been cheating on me*, I thought. Perhaps they already knew; they might even have met Clare.

My memories poured out again.

I could never pull off your outfit, Clare.

I squashed them down by packing each memory into a box and storing it at the back of my mind. But with each passing moment, it got harder and harder to keep the memories filed away. The stack of imaginary boxes wobbled and grew, threatening to tumble over and release my memories until there was nothing I could do to stop it, until there was nothing left of me but that day.

I'd had enough of standing and waiting. I took matters into my own hands once his parents left, and I stalked over to the bed. I placed one hand over James's chest and yelled at him to wake up, then I whacked him with my handbag for good measure.

What I never expected was for my bag to actually touch him, causing everything to fall out, onto the floor. As I scrambled to pick the items up, the monitors in the room started to beep faster and faster until he flatlined. Alarms rang out, and I crawled back to the corner to evade the barrage of doctors and nurses who ran in with a crash cart.

'Oh, shit, I've killed the bastard!' I whispered. 'I'm done for, now.'

'Caroline,' a hollow, haunted voice called out to me.

'Huh?' I cast my eyes around the room.

'Caroline,' it called again.

I glanced up to the ceiling; James's spirit looked down on me, and not a copy of the body in the bed, but fresh as a daisy, dressed in a suit.

'Oh, Caroline, I've been so lost. Where have you been? Why am I floating?' He glanced down. 'Oh shit, is that me down there?' His mouth opened in a giant O.

Below him, doctors and nurses worked on his body, shouting orders, and pumping him with medication and electricity.

In his confused state, mumbled questions poured from his spirit's mouth. But my needs were greater. I ignored his questions and pressed on with my own.

'Look, James, I don't have much time. I'll get to the point. I know what you've been doing with that tramp, Clare.'

He froze, and his face dropped. 'Clare? No, no, you've got it all wrong—'

'Save the pleading for someone else. I want to know what happened to my car. I'm dead, and I deserve to know why,' I demanded.

'Don't be stupid, you're not dead. What have I told you about your theatrics?' James looked back at his body. 'What are they doing? What's going on?'

I clicked my fingers twice. 'James, focus, please!'

His eyes snapped back to mine. 'Caroline, there you are. Where have you been?'

I frowned. *What?* 'James, do you remember we were in an accident?'

'An accident?' His faced screwed up in confusion.

'Yes, you were driving. There was something wrong with the brakes. Did you loosen them?'

'I couldn't brake,' he whispered.

'That's right. Did you do something to the car, James?'

He shook his head madly. 'Me? No!'

Seeing the horror on his face made me realise it couldn't have been James. Why would a person tamper with a car, then willingly get in the driver's seat? It made no sense.

The bustle in the room died down, and I knew I didn't have long left. Either they would save James, or they would call it, and he would disappear.

'Well, do you know who did? Come on, think. Did someone want to hurt you?'

'Hurt me?' he said.

'Yes! Come on, James. You've been lying to me for god knows how long. I really need honesty right now!' I pleaded.

'Clare…' he whispered.

'Yes, you and Clare had an affair.' Then I muttered, 'Rub it in, why don't you?'

'I wanted to end it.'

'And?' I coaxed.

'She said she'd hurt you if I ended it.'

I launched up from the floor. 'What!'

'She wanted to hurt you.'

'And you never thought to tell me?' I whispered shaking my head.

CHAPTER FIFTEEN

I've got a promotion. Wahoo!

One of the memories had toppled over. I wrestled with it and pushed it back. I had one last question to ask.

'James, do you have a secret stash of money I don't know about?'

'Yes... I have a trust from my grandad. I get the money on my thirtieth...' He trailed off and turned his face away.

'You're a liar and a cheat James,' I said lowering my head.

James uttered inaudible words before his spirit floated back into his body and the monitors and machines fell back into their normal rhythm. All of the doctors and nurses filed out except for one who updated James's chart. She remained for a moment, checking the machines, then she left.

I paced the floor to process James's revelation; Clare had wanted to hurt me. I had to be sure she was responsible, and I had to be quick.

The danger I faced was edging nearer, and I needed help. I fought harder than I'd ever fought for anything to ensure the memories stopped leaking out so I could concentrate.

There were only two people capable of helping me now: Tamara and Eliza. If anyone could convince Clare to fess up it would be her.

* * *

Eliza sat colouring at a little table while Tamara stared at her laptop at the breakfast bar with a mug in her hands. I walked across the room silently and crouched by the little girl.

'Eliza,' I whispered.

'Aunty Caz!' she squealed and leapt up, sending crayons scattering to the floor.

Tamara jumped and spilt her drink over her laptop. 'Oh damn, Eliza, don't lie to mummy. Is Caroline really here?' she said as she ran for a cloth.

'Mummy, you said a naughty word.'

'I know, I'm sorry, but sometimes adults accidentally say things they don't mean. Do you understand?' she asked gently as she mopped the laptop, her eyes focused on Eliza.

Eliza nodded.

Tamara knelt down in front of her. 'Now, I want you to be honest with me. Did you say something you didn't mean to say?'

'No, Mummy.'

'Is Caroline really here?' Tamara pressed on with her questioning.

Perhaps she hadn't believed David the medium when he had told her Eliza had seen me, or she just didn't want to.

'Yes, Mummy.' Eliza giggled as she picked up the crayons.

Though Eliza was only four, she wasn't a messy child.

Tamara frowned and got back to her feet. She continued to wipe the spill, though I was certain she'd got it all.

'Eliza, can you tell your mum I need her help,' I said, remaining eye level with her.

'Mummy, Aunty Caz said she needs help.' Her brow furrowed as she focused on putting her crayons back in a row.

'Okay.' Tamara slumped onto the stool behind her and dropped the cloth on the tiled floor.

'She said okay, Aunty Caz,' relayed an eager Eliza, now finished with her task.

'It's alright, Eliza, I can hear her, but she can't hear or see me. Do you understand?'

She nodded, a grin plastered to her angelic face. She looked from me to her mum. 'Mummy, are you going to help Aunty Caz?' she asked.

'Just a minute, Eliza, I'm thinking,' she said, blinking fast and running a hand through her thick, chestnut hair.

I knew exactly what would be running through Tamara's mind; how the hell was I stood in her kitchen?

As the room remained silent except for the whirr of the washing machine, I looked at their faces and pictured us standing in the same spots, baking, our faces covered in flour and icing.

'Okay,' Tamara finally composed herself. 'I want Caroline to tell me something only me and her would know.' She glanced around, seemingly trying to figure out where I was.

I moved from Eliza's side to Tamara's and placed my hand over her right shin. 'Eliza, ask your mum if she can feel something on her leg.'

'Okay. Mummy, can you feel something on your leg?' Eliza swayed side to side in anticipation.

Tamara frowned and ran a hand down her jeans, stopping where my hand lay. 'It feels a bit cold, why?' she questioned.

'Tell her it's where she hurt it the night we pushed each other around in shopping trollies.'

'Silly Aunty Caz,' she giggled.

'I know.' I smiled. 'Go on, tell her.'

'Aunty Caz said it's where you hurt your leg.' She paused to look at me. 'I forgot.'

'It's okay, sweetie. The night we pushed each other in trollies.'

'The night you pushed trollies!' she said excitedly and clapped her little hands.

Tamara gasped and brought her hand to her mouth. 'Caroline, are you really here?' she whispered.

'Tell her yes.'

'Yes, Mummy, she's right there.' Eliza pointed at me.

Tamara sat up, tears pooling in her eyes. She reached a trembling hand out for me, then quickly pulled it back. 'Caroline?' she whispered again.

I hugged her. Though I know she couldn't feel it, I hoped it made her feel better.

'What... can I do?' she asked.

I wilted with relief that she was going to help. I smiled at Eliza who smiled back at us.

'Ask your mum to move the laptop so I can write something for her.'

I didn't want to move it myself—who knows how much I'd scare Eliza. Though at this point, I doubted anything fazed this child.

Tamara moved the laptop and loaded up a writing programme for me. I found the strength to type out a message for Tamara. The duo watched in amazement as words filled the screen.

'Tamara, I don't have much time to explain. My death wasn't an accident. Someone tampered with my car, and I think Clare had something to do with it.'

'Your manager Clare?' asked Tamara.

'Yes. I need you to confront her. You're the only person I know who can do this for me.'

'H-how am I going to do that?' she stammered.

'What does it say, Mummy?' Eliza interrupted.

'It's adult talk, sweetheart. Why don't you go finish your colouring in, okay?'

Eliza skipped back to her paper and crayons, unaffected by

CHAPTER FIFTEEN

what was taking place.

'*I have an idea,*' I typed. '*You need to invite her for a drink or something. Tell her you want the shoes under my desk. Say I promised them to you. They're probably still there.*'

'Okay. I can handle that.' She took a deep breath. 'I've handled worse things.'

'*Good. Call her. Now!*'

Tamara scrambled for her phone. 'Wait a second. Why do you think it was Clare?'

'*Clare and James were having an affair. She was also after his money.*'

'What the fudge? What money?'

I laughed at her choice of expression as I recalled the hours we'd spent coming up with alternative phrases in preparation for Eliza's first words.

'Mummy, you were going to a say another naughty word!' Eliza shouted over, still colouring away. She was as bright as a star and never missed a trick.

'*TRUST FUND,*' I typed out.

'Sorry, Eliza. Caroline, are you sure?'

'*V. sure. Call her quickly. Put it on speaker.*'

Tamara dialled, then placed the phone on the table.

'Revelation Consulting, can I help you?' the receptionist sang.

'Clare Jollands, please?'

'May I ask who is calling?'

'Tell her it's Tamara Fairbanks; she knows who I am,' she said firmly.

'One moment, please.'

Classical music played through the speakers, then the phone clicked as it connected to Clare.

'Tamara, darling, I've not spoken with you since Caroline's memorial. How are you keeping? Dating yet?'

Ouch, that had to sting, I thought.

'Not bad, Clare,' Tamara said calmly, not reacting to the comment.

'What can I do for you?'

I've got a promotion. Wahoo! My memories started to replay again, though I was thankful I'd kept them away long enough to get the help I needed.

'Just a small favour. Caroline left a pair of shoes under her desk. She always promised I could have them, but she never got round to it. I was wondering if they were still there.'

'Well, yes, they are. I have all her belongings here. No one has been for them and I forgot to mention it at the memorial. But I'm not so sure I should hand them over to just anyone.'

'Come on, Clare, I'm not just anyone. Caroline and I were friends for years, and that loser James won't be collecting them anytime soon.'

Nice dig, Tamara. Two thumbs up.

Tamara smiled, and if the dig got to Clare, she didn't react either.

'Umm…'

'Please, Clare, it's…' She sighed and sniffed, though her face showed little of the emotion her voice was portraying. 'It's something to remember her by.'

I smirked at Tamara's act, and after a moment of silence, Clare groaned lightly.

'Fine, you've won me over. Just the shoes, though.'

'Great, you don't know what this means to me. I was thinking we could meet for a drink and you could bring them?'

'Umm, let me see… I'm pretty tied up this week. I can meet

CHAPTER FIFTEEN

you in half an hour, if that works?'

Why can't I get hold of James? For some reason, the memories only trickled out now. I clung on to the hope that Tamara would get to the bottom of it all.

'Sure thing. At Tooley's?'

'See you there.'

Clare ended the call before Tamara could say anything else.

'Now what?' asked Tamara.

'Talk to her. I know you can make her spill her guts. Please!'

'Okay, okay.' She took another deep breath. 'I can do this. Eliza, run and grab your shoes and mac. Do you fancy a playdate at Billy's?'

'Yay!' she yelled and ran off.

'I'll wait for you in Tooley's,' I typed out, then I left.

* * *

Across the road from where I used to work stood Tooley's bar. It was a little bar we frequented on the odd occasion.

Clare arrived first and ordered a large glass of Pinot noir. She sat in a booth near the entrance. She didn't look her normal cheery self. Her hair had lost its normal bounce, and her eyes were sunken.

Tell Eliza I love her.

Tamara arrived a few moments later. She slipped into the booth after ordering a coke, and I slid in beside her. I gave her hand a squeeze, which made her shiver.

'You alright, Tamara?' asked Clare.

'Fine, just a bit chilly.'

Clare pushed the shoebox across the table. 'Here're the shoes you asked for.'

'Great.' Tamara peered inside, then closed the lid.

Roses. It's not a special occasion, is it?

They sat in awkward silence. Tamara tapped nervously on the table until Clare cleared her throat.

'How have you been keeping?' she asked.

'Good. You?'

'Good.' Clare nodded.

'Hmm, very awkward,' I muttered and squeezed Tamara's hand again. 'You can do this Tamara. I know you can.'

Tamara took a deep breath. 'There is another reason I wanted to meet up.'

Clare cocked her head. 'Really? Why? Do you need me to get you a date? I've got loads of numbers,' she said, reaching for her phone.

Tamara shook her head and took another deep breath. 'Rumour has it you had an affair with James,' she said, not taking her eyes off Clare's face.

Who's CJ?

Clare's expression barely moved except for the tiniest twitch at the corner of her mouth. It made me think Tamara and Clare might have been a good poker team in another world. She started to run her finger around the rim of her wine glass, then smiled.

'You know rumours are spread by fools, Tamara.'

'Yes, and accepted by idiots. And I'm neither, Clare. I have a reliable source.'

Clare laughed, throwing her head back, then composed herself. 'Let me guess, that bitch Sophia. I don't know what lies, she's been spreading, but—'

'Caroline,' Tamara whispered, interrupting Clare's rambling.

Wow, so it would seem Sophia did have something on Clare.

CHAPTER FIFTEEN

Clare's face dropped at the sound of my name. 'Caroline?' she scoffed.

'You heard me. Caroline told me.'

We're going out for steak to celebrate.

'She knew?' Clare whispered as the colour drained from her face.

'No, but she does now,' Tamara replied.

'What do you mean now?' she spluttered. 'What game are you trying to pull?'

'No game.' Tamara reached out and dug her expertly French-manicured nails into Clare's hand, causing the woman to cry out in pain. 'Don't make a scene, Clare.'

'Bitch, get off me, you're hurting me!' Clare said through clenched teeth.

'Did you cause Caroline's accident?'

Clare didn't answer. Tamara dug her nails in harder.

Why is the car spinning?

'Ouch! Are you nuts?' Clare groaned.

'Tell me. I can sit like this all night,' Tamara snapped.

And then Clare broke down. I imagined the weeks of carrying the burden, plus whatever else she had going on, had taken its toll on her.

'I didn't mean for it to happen the way it did,' she sobbed. 'I only wanted her out of commission for a few weeks so I could convince James not to leave me.'

'Go on,' urged Tamara. 'What did you do?'

'I arranged for someone to tamper with Caroline's car.'

The memories stopped replaying. The world brightened. I felt light and free.

'I didn't know they would both be in it.' She continued to sob. 'I didn't expect her to die—she was my friend, too.'

'What did you think would happen, you stupid cow?' Tamara spat.

A glass smashed behind us. Tamara flinched and glanced over her shoulder, causing her to lose the grip she had on Clare's hand.

Clare took the chance to escape; she snatched her bag and ran out of the bar.

'Shoot,' Tamara uttered and ran off behind her. I followed, but she came to a stop just beyond the doors.

'Caroline,' she sighed, 'if you're still here, I'm sorry. I can't run in these heels.'

I gave her hand a parting squeeze, then left her side and legged it after Clare. Man, could she run fast in heels; I was surprised she didn't topple over and break her ankle.

I finally caught up with her as she turned down an alleyway. She had slowed to the same half-run I saw her do in the supermarket.

I kept a steady pace behind her, wondering what she was about to do next. I had to keep an eye on her and make sure she faced up to what she had done.

'There you are,' a male voice said behind me.

I turned around with a witty retort ready, expecting to find Eisen stood behind me, but instead, a brute of a man towered over me—the same brute George and I had seen at her door. But he wasn't looking at me; he was staring *through* me.

I looked back to Clare who had frozen to the spot.

'You can't run now, bitch,' he spat. 'Didn't I tell you not to hang up on me?'

He started to march towards her, his giant feet clunking on the tarmac. He walked straight through me with no recognition of the shiver he must have felt.

CHAPTER FIFTEEN

Clare turned around, clutching something in her right hand.

'Don't come any closer,' she stammered. 'I've got pepper spray!'

'What the heck?' I yelled.

Who was this man and what did he want with Clare?

The brute laughed. 'No, you don't,' he said, grabbing her wrist, causing her to drop the small bottle of perfume she had been holding.

He roughly pushed her into a nearby giant refuse bin.

'Get off me!' Clare yelled.

'Save it, blondie. No one is coming to save you,' he said, glancing up and down the alley. 'Mr Matthews is extremely unhappy with you. He expects payment—in full. Tomorrow. Do you understand?' he said an inch from her face.

'Wow, Clare! You have got yourself into a little mess, haven't you?' I said.

'But… I can't,' Clare hesitated.

'What did you say?'

'I-I thought I'd get the money from my boyfriend, but he was involved in a crash, and I-I don't know—'

The brute grabbed Clare around the neck.

'Oh shit!' I yelled.

Clare grappled with the brute and pulled at his fingers. Her face turned red as she struggled to breathe.

I had a decision to make, and fast. I could watch as the brute choked her, possibly to death, or I could save her, despite all she had done.

Not helping her wasn't me, and I scanned the vicinity for something I could use to get him off her, spotting a small plank of wood.

I picked it up and swiped the back of his legs. He didn't

budge or flinch. So I tried a second time.

'Oi!' he said and looked behind him.

I obviously hadn't hurt him, but the action had been enough for him to release her. Clare seized the chance to escape and ran back down the alley.

I was happy to let her go as I stood and watched the brute scratch his head as he looked at the plank at his feet.

When I was satisfied, he would be leaving Clare alone for now, I went back to Tamara's to leave a note on her abandoned laptop, thanking her for her help:

Tamara,

Thank you for helping me. You should know I'm at peace now. Don't worry that you couldn't chase her. I caught up with her just before she was accosted by some sort of debt collector.

I also need to apologise, for using Eliza to communicate with you. I hope you can forgive me.

I've left this feather for you. If you ever find one in the future, it means I'm close by.

Caroline xo

Chapter Sixteen

Safe in the knowledge I wouldn't be losing myself anytime soon, I went to find Daniel where we first met and found him sat on a bench, reading the paper of the man sat next to him.

'Hey, some people consider that rude, you know.'

'Hi, Caroline,' he said without looking at me.

'Are you okay?'

He continued to read the paper. 'Yep, fine.'

'You could at least look at me when I'm talking to you. Do you have any idea what I've just been through?'

He sighed and buried his face in his hands. 'I'm sorry, I just didn't expect to see you again.'

I moved in front of him. 'What do you mean?'

'I thought I'd lost you to your memories.'

I pulled his hands from his face and sat on his lap.

'I'd resigned myself to being on my own again,' he continued.

I tutted. 'You daft sod, did you really have no faith in me?'

'I always have faith in you. I just didn't have any in the situation you found yourself in. I felt so helpless here waiting for you. I haven't moved from this spot.'

I rolled my eyes at his melodrama. 'Daniel, it's over now. I'm back, and I don't plan on leaving your side ever again. I found out who was responsible. You know my manager who had an affair with my husband?'

He nodded.

'Well, it was down to her. It seems as though she was in loads of debt and needed James's money. Apparently, he's got a secret stash I never knew about.' I shrugged.

'Wow…' he said. 'I mean, I'm sorry it all happened, but… wow.' Then he kissed me and whispered close to my lips, 'I missed you so much.'

'I missed you too. It wasn't an experience I wish to repeat. I fought so hard to keep the memories from engulfing me so I could get back to you.'

'Are you sure the matter is resolved?' he asked as he stroked my hair.

'I think so. For me it is anyway. I mean, I know she did it. I could feel it; there was a moment when she broke down, and everything I'd been battling just fluttered away. All I felt was peace. It's up to the police to deal with now,' I told him.

Daniel tilted his head and looked me straight in the eye. 'What if they don't?'

'I'm sure she'll be on her way to see them now. She was attacked. I had to save her from this giant brute. Plus, James knew she wanted to hurt me and—'

His eyebrows raised. 'She was attacked? And how did you find out James knew?'

'Yes, after Tamara got her to confess, she ran off, and a man followed her. He tried to choke her and… Well, I stopped him.'

'You did? And James?' he asked.

'Well, short story… I think he had a heart attack. His spirit left his body, but it didn't leave—it just floated near the ceiling. I spoke to him. He told me Clare wanted to hurt me.'

CHAPTER SIXTEEN

'Oh-kay...'

'And Tamara knows,' I repeated. 'She can tell them, and if James wakes up, so can he.'

'What if they don't believe her, Caroline? Or he doesn't wake up? What then? We need to do something.' He tipped me off his lap and stood up.

'But what can we do? I promised I'd never get revenge.'

'I don't know yet. What about this George you mentioned? Surely he has information on her we can use.'

'I don't know about this, Daniel. Are you really sure this is the path we should be taking? I can't use what I've learnt to hurt her. Evidently she's got enough problems.'

'I don't want to hurt her, either. I'm out of that game. I had to leave Jane because of her insidious actions. But there must be some way of making sure Clare hands herself in.'

I shook my head. 'Okay...' I sighed. 'I'll go down this road with you. But you've got to promise me we're not going to hurt her.'

'Promise,' he said. 'Scouts honour.'

'I didn't know you were in the Scouts.'

'There's a lot you don't know, kid.' He winked.

We arrived in Clare's kitchen, and I called out for George, hoping Michael hadn't been to collect him.

'Caroline, is that you?' he said, walking in from the living room. 'And you've brought a friend this time, how lovely,' he added.

'George, this is Daniel.'

'Pleased to meet you, Daniel. Any friend of Caroline's is a friend of mine.'

'Nice to meet you too, sir,' said Daniel.

'So, Caroline, is this Daniel the reason you've not stopped

by for a visit?'

'He is George,' I laughed.

'Now, what can I do for you both?' George asked.

'George, did you see Clare after she finished work?' I asked him.

'Nope, she's not been home yet. My, she is popular today, though.'

'Popular how?'

'This morning, the same thuggish bloke we saw knocked at the door for ages. He even crept round the back and looked through the windows, the cheeky beggar.'

I turned to Daniel. 'That's the same guy who attacked her.'

'Clare was attacked?' asked George. 'Caroline, what's going on?'

'I was hoping you'd be able to tell me.'

George rubbed a hand across his forehead. 'Tell you what?'

'Clare arranged for my car to be tampered with. That's why I died.'

'She did what!' George rumbled. Glasses started to shake, and the pots and pans rattled.

'Calm down, George,' Daniel soothed, placing a placating hand on the old man's shoulder. The crockery stilled.

'I'm sorry. I've always kept my emotions under control,' George sighed. 'I can't believe she did that. I knew she was a bit unstable, but this? Beggars belief…' George sat on a stool at the breakfast bar, and I perched next to him.

'Did you really not know she was like this?'

'No. I've tried my best not to listen to her goings on. It's not my business, after all.' He shook his head.

'I understand. But is there anything you can think of that may help? Anything at all?'

CHAPTER SIXTEEN

'I've heard her threaten people before,' he sighed. 'I thought she was all mouth and no trousers. I never once thought she was serious.'

'Perhaps she's done this more than once,' I said to Daniel.

He shrugged. 'It's possible.'

'George, do you know of any places she likes to go?'

'Not really. From what I can tell, all she does right now is go to work, the hospital now and again, and her regular nights out with whomever she is courting.'

'The hospital? Daniel, she might have gone to see James. Maybe we can track her down there.'

'You aren't going to hurt her, are you, Caroline?' George asked. 'Remember what you promised me.'

'No—'

'We need to make sure she either hands herself in or the police find her,' Daniel interrupts me, and I shrugged.

'And how you going to do that?' George enquired.

'Maybe I can help?' My gran stepped out from behind Daniel.

'Gran! What are you doing here?'

She smiled. 'I told you I'd see you again.'

'Gran, do you know what I found out today?' I said, giving her a hug.

'Bits and bobs, yes.' She turned to Daniel. 'Lovely to meet you, Daniel, finally.'

'You too. I feel like I already know you.' He laughed. 'Caroline completely adores you.'

Gran smiled and nodded. 'I know. But we don't have much time for chit chat and pleasantries. We've got to do something to ensure Clare gets her just desserts.'

'I don't know about this, Gran,' I said. 'I feel as though she will get that through her conscience, and I'm fine with that.'

'No, Caroline, you don't deserve to be here. I want to make sure she does the right thing,' she said, taking a stance like she was ready for a fight.

I never thought my Gran would want to seek revenge; I'd never seen this side of her.

'Gran, as much as I can see your point, I feel as though I was meant to be here. I don't know why,' I said, grabbing Daniel's hand and giving it a squeeze.

'No, Caroline,' she said, her face grim.

I sighed and relented. 'What can we do, Gran?'

'I think, if we work as a collective, we should have enough influence to nudge Clare onto the right path of handing herself in. It will take the four of us.'

'Four?' interrupted George.

'Yes, you too,' Gran informed him.

George shook his head. 'I don't know if I should be getting involved.' He rose from the stool. 'I've only got two days left here. I don't want to be getting into trouble.'

'Then that's all the reason you need to do it. Leave on a high, knowing you've done something good,' said Gran.

'Please, George,' Daniel said.

George looked down at his feet. 'I'm a little rusty,' he sighed.

'To the hospital we go. Hold hands, everyone!' I shouted.

The four of us fumbled for each other's hands, resulting in a few laughs. It took longer than I anticipated to get to the hospital. When I'd gone anywhere with Daniel, I left all the travelling to him. I surprised myself, though; I was able to transport us all there without incident.

At the hospital, we found James had woken from his coma, and he was in the middle of an argument with Clare.

'I won't ask you again, Clare,' James croaked. 'Where is

Caroline?'

Tears filled her eyes. 'Calm down, James, you've had a terrible knock to the head. I'll go fetch someone.'

'Stay right there!' he spat. 'I asked you a question. Tell me what I want to—' He spluttered and coughed, his command dying with the action.

'You need some water,' she said, reaching for a nearby beaker to bring to his lips. James swiped it from her hand, sending it to the floor.

'Answer me!' he shouted.

'Caro...' Clare gulped. 'Caroline died.'

James's faced scrunched up in torment. 'Get out!' he yelled.

'James you're in shock, you've just woken up. You don't know what you're saying. I'll go fetch a doctor,' Clare said and ran out.

'Check she's not running off,' said Gran.

'Okay,' I left the room and looked for Clare. She was stood at the nurse's station, demanding a doctor see James. She brought back a doctor and a nurse.

The room was cramped now; the four of us spirits huddled together in a corner, watching the scene unfold.

'Mr Rushton, I'm Dr Barnard. Can you tell me your full name?' he asked.

'Yes, James Francis Rushton.'

'Good, and your date of birth?'

'Fifteen, two, ninety.'

'Good. Now, you've only been awake a couple of hours. It's quite normal to feel overwhelmed and confused.'

'I'm fine,' said James. 'Dr Barnard, could you kindly get me the police?'

'The police? James,' Clare pleaded, 'you don't know what

you are saying. You're confused. Listen to the doctor.'

'I'm not confused. And you need to get out. Now!' He slammed his hand down on the overbed table.

The doctor stepped forwards. 'If you wouldn't mind stepping outside, miss. Are you even a relative?' Dr Barnard questioned, then glanced at the nurse as though she should have queried Clare's presence.

'Yes. No, but...' Clare stuttered and looked for help from the nurse.

The nurse cleared her throat and reached for the notes at the foot of the bed, ignoring her pleading eyes.

'Then perhaps you should leave, or I'll have to call security. Nurse Taylor if you wouldn't mind,' said the doctor.

The nurse put back the notes and took Clare by the elbow, ushering her into the corridor. We trundled after them in single file, then formed a circle outside the room.

I watched Clare as she hurried down the corridor and disappeared around the corner. The nurse returned to her station.

George shook his head slowly as he also watched her vanish.

'What should we do, Gran?' I asked as I entwined Daniel's hand with mine.

I could hear James reasoning with the doctor, insisting he called the police for him.

'Nothing. I think James will make sure the police know what she did,' Gran said, her eyes on his room.

'You think so?' I asked as I chewed on my lip.

'Of course,' she said, now focusing on me. 'How do you feel, Caroline? Do you feel as though you might lose yourself? Are you confident you know what happened to you?'

'I feel great, Gran. Even before we came here. You know,

CHAPTER SIXTEEN

considering...'

'Then there is no need to intercede,' she said.

'What? No chase? No epic battle between good and evil?' asked Daniel as he pretended to do a karate chop. I laughed.

Gran shook her head. 'Not today, my dears.'

The doctor exited James's room. We all had the same thought and quickly moved aside to let him pass. I feared it would be too much for him to pass through four spirits at once.

'Does this mean I can go?' asked George as he shuffled his feet.

'Yes. Thanks, George,' I reached for his hand, and he smiled. 'Sorry for dragging you into all this.'

'Don't worry your pretty little head, Caroline. It's been my pleasure,' he said and placed his other hand over mine.

'Say hello to your wife for me,' I told him.

'I will.' George waved, then left.

I sighed. 'Are you going too, Gran?'

'Yes. It seems I wasn't needed, after all.'

'I'll always need you, Gran,' I whispered into her hair as I hugged her goodbye.

'I know, dear,' she said and disappeared.

'So...' said Daniel.

'So?' I replied.

'Do you want to say goodbye to James?'

I peeped round the door at the man I used to love. He sat propped in his bed with his head in his hands. 'No,' I answered.

'No?' he questioned. 'Better things to do?' His eyebrow raised.

I nodded. 'Better things to do.'

Chapter Seventeen

After the time we'd spent apart, Daniel and I had a lot of catching up to do. I filled him in fully on all that had happened, then we resumed our wild ride of adventure and romance.

I use the term *romance* loosely. Daniel wasn't a romantic person; how could he be? He couldn't nip into a shop and buy me gifts. He didn't recite poetry or send me love letters. He hadn't even said the three words I longed to hear.

When I look back, none of that mattered, anyway. We had the world to explore, conversations to hold, and each other. We met other spirits on our journey who seemed surprised that our relationship worked. Although we were not far apart in age, we had been born decades apart and we had little in common. But their comments didn't bother us; we did work, and we were happy.

In October, we arrived in Paris on Friday the thirteenth.

The sun shined and many people took advantage of the autumnal weather. Daniel and I strolled amongst the Parisians and tourists along the bank of the Seine. We glanced at prints and paintings on the artists' stalls; I enjoyed watching the painters bring canvas and colour to life.

Daniel's expression appeared distant, however. He didn't

CHAPTER SEVENTEEN

seem to be relishing the scene as much as I was.

'What's up with you today? Not getting bored of me, are you?' I asked, gently nudging him with my elbow.

'Of course not, why would you ask that? I'm just tired.'

'Daniel, we don't get tired. We have no need for sleep,' I chided him.

He just shrugged in response.

Paranoia swooped in, and I pondered if he really had become bored with me. Perhaps, we'd moved too fast in our relationship. But I brushed the doubts away. Despite how much I'd grown with Daniel, I was still naïve to clues staring me in the face.

'Another river ticked off the list,' said Daniel, changing the subject when we got as far as we could walk along the bank.

'Yep; how many is that now?' I asked.

'Seventeen.'

'Wow, I couldn't even name ten till I met you,' I laughed.

Daniel smiled. 'Where to now?'

'I've always wanted to see Oscar Wilde's grave, and Jim Morrison's. I'm sure they're buried in the same cemetery.'

'Alright, babe. But you know it's going to be inundated with other spirits and faceless ones. Have you forgotten that incident in Arlington already?'

I hadn't forgotten at all, and I didn't want a repeat either.

The incident had happened three weeks earlier. We had started the day in the Pentagon, listening in on secret meetings and looking through confidential archives, though the documents were heavily redacted; it seemed a pointless task to me.

'I'm bored now,' Daniel sighed. 'I can't find what I'm looking for. We could spend weeks here and still not find it.'

I had no idea what he had been looking for, and I never asked. Though he'd told me about his theories, the majority went straight over my head.

'Okay, anywhere else you want to go?' I asked.

'Well, seeing as it's across the way, we may as well visit Arlington Cemetery,' he said sheepishly.

I knew our next destination would be the cemetery; I could read him like a book. As soon as we arrived in Washington, I knew there'd be no chance he could pass up the opportunity to see J.F.K.'s grave.

I smirked. 'Sure, babe. Anything you want.'

Daniel put his arms around my waist, and we landed in front of J.F.K.'s memorial. I stepped back a few paces to let him pay his respects and glanced to my left, spotting a few people roaming around. I turned back to Daniel as he began to recite the Lord's Prayer, and when I bowed my head, a large black mitten grabbed my arm.

I looked up to shout at my accoster, but instead of a face, I was confronted with darkness. Then I was stood in my parent's garden. The shock of staring into a black circle of what should have been a face had transported me away. I'd seen many faceless ones since my first experience with my gran, but never close up.

Everywhere we went, they seemed to gravitate towards me, but this was my first close up encounter. I recalled Eisen's first conversation with me and wondered if this was the change he'd referred to.

I stayed in my parent's garden with my fingers crossed, hoping it wouldn't take Daniel long to locate me.

'What happened?' Daniel exclaimed, pulling me into a hug when he finally did.

CHAPTER SEVENTEEN

I buried my head in his chest. 'A faceless one grabbed me.'

He kissed the top of my head. 'Oh, sweetheart.'

'I'm okay, I think. It caught me off guard, that's all, and I ended up here.'

'I bet it did. You know they probably only wanted your help.'

'I guess so. I wish I knew how to help them,' I sighed. 'Do you want to go back?' I asked him.

'No, I've said what I wanted to say and seen all I can for now.'

'Good. Where now?'

He smiled that mischievous grin I loved so much. 'How about Wyoming?'

'Wyoming?' I quirked an eyebrow. 'What's in Wyoming?'

He winked. 'You'll see.'

I wasn't certain I wouldn't have another experience like that one, but I promised Daniel I'd keep my wits about me as we went to Oscar Wilde's grave. I recounted one of his quotes, then we weaved through the cemetery to Jim Morrison's final resting place.

'I would never have pegged you as a Doors fan,' said Daniel.

'Hah, blame my parents for that. They have an eclectic taste in music. I grew up listening to all sorts.'

'They've got good taste.'

'I know.' I tugged his arm so he had to walk quicker. I'd spotted a couple of faceless ones and didn't want them to head our way. At least not until I had figured out how to help them. I hadn't told Daniel that it had been playing on my mind for months that there must be something we—or I—could do.

As we approached the grave, I started to sing one of The Doorses' songs, and Daniel joined in at the chorus. I paid my respects, then we left in a hurry.

Daniel had never ridden on the metro before. We jumped

on at Pere Lachaise Station and rode the lines until we arrived at Republique.

Daniel picked the stop because he liked the name. I told him I did the same when I picked horses for the Grand National. He laughed and said he learnt new things about me every day.

We exited the station onto a large square; a stage had been erected at one end, and at the other, technician's fixed lights to rigging.

'Cool, my first open air concert!' said Daniel, he picked me up and twirled me around. 'Can we stay?'

I laughed at his eagerness. 'Sure. Have you never been to a concert before?'

'Of course, I have. Not outside, though.'

'You'll love it.'

'I hope it starts soon,' Daniel said with a tone of sadness which appeared from nowhere.

A mariachi band appeared on stage and conducted a sound-check. Daniel and I sat on some steps to people-watch while we waited for the concert to start.

A strange electricity built up and hung in the air. It made me uncomfortable. Daniel shrugged it off when I mentioned it, claiming it was nothing to worry about. So we sat in silence until the electricity increased to a point where I wanted to be sick. I hadn't had this feeling since my funeral.

'Can you not that feel that?' I asked Daniel.

'No,' he muttered.

Out of nowhere, the yells of angry men erupted in the air all around us. We jumped to our feet and looked for the source. No one else noticed the commotion.

'Over there.' Daniel pointed to the opposite side of the square.

CHAPTER SEVENTEEN

We ran towards the shouts. Men were dressed in old-fashioned armour and were brandishing swords. They were running in all directions, pointing and yelling in French.

'Is it a battle re-enactment?'

'No, look,' said Daniel. 'No one is taking any notice. They're spirits.'

'What—all of them?' I left Daniel and moved closer as I realised I recognised a sole bystander watching the men as they huddled together. 'It can't be...' I whispered. 'What's *he* doing here?'

Daniel moved to my side. 'What's wrong?' he asked.

'That's Eisen,' I said. 'What's he up to?' I uttered and walked over to him. The group dispersed, spread out, and adopted a fighting stance.

'What are you doing here, Eisen? Are you still following me?' I asked.

'No, watch.' He pointed to the other spirits.

Max, the man I'd observed in the woods with Eisen, appeared. His clothes had changed now. He wore an old-fashioned mantle with a cross on the front. The other spirits roared and ran forwards, encircling Max. Before I could shout a warning, they attacked him. No one came to his aid. I attempted to run to him, but Eisen held me back.

'Get off me!' I yelled.

'You can't help him,' he said as I struggled against his grasp. 'This happened to him hundreds of years ago. It has to play out,' said Eisen.

'Oh god,' I said and turned away as the men dragged Max's body down the square.

'It's over,' he whispered, then released me.

I turned to face him. 'Why didn't you help him?' I demanded.

'The past is the past. It can't be altered in any way or form.'

'You're still talking in riddles! You were his guide, and you let him die?' I snarled.

'He didn't die then. He lived for many years after that. That was a small snippet of his life.'

'Huh?'

'Max was a Knight Templar. They were wrongly persecuted. Moments like the one you just witnessed replay all over the city every Friday the Thirteenth of October. Max's soul has been reborn many times, through many generations. He still lives on,' he said, then walked away.

I stood staring after him but lost him in the crowd.

Yet again, he'd left me puzzled. I still wasn't clear on why he'd taken me to see him all those months ago. I always felt like Eisen was on the verge of telling me more or wanting to ask me something, but he always changed his mind. Like he was waiting for me to piece it all together and tell him.

'What was all that about? Are you okay? I lost you in the crowd and—Caroline are you listening to me?' Daniel asked, gently holding my face in his hands.

'Yes... Yes, I'm fine.' I checked behind me. I couldn't be sure he had really gone. 'I've just spoken to Eisen, the spirit guide I met months ago. I don't want to alarm you, but I think he needs me to help with something, for some reason he's reluctant to tell me what it is yet.'

'Really? Where is he? I'll have a word,' Daniel said, looking over my head.

I shook my head. 'He's gone.'

'Well, that was some fight,' he said.

'Listen, Daniel, the man they dragged away... I've seen him before.'

CHAPTER SEVENTEEN

'That's impossible. He's clearly a spirit from centuries ago.'

'I have. Eisen took me to the past, and I saw him there. We're connected somehow, I don't know...' I trailed off and shook my head again.

Daniel puffed out his cheeks. 'Beats me. Are you sure you'll be okay?'

'Yes, I'll be fine.'

'Good, because I want to dance with you. Just forget what you saw and come be with me.'

I nodded, but I couldn't forget it. It just didn't make sense.

Eisen had taken me to see Max for a reason, and it couldn't be a coincidence that I'd chosen Paris to visit today and witness those events. There had to be a connection between the two.

I let Daniel lead me back across the square. I hadn't heard the music start as I'd watched the awful scene unfold.

A crowd had gathered in the square, and a few couples danced, including us. After a few songs, the tempo slowed, and the band played a familiar tune, though they kept repeating the intro until a tall man appeared on stage with a tambourine and wearing an oversized sombrero. The man started to sing.

'I know this song.' I grinned. 'It's a Morrissey song. He has a huge following in Mexico, you know.'

'Really?' Daniel laughed. 'You never fail to amaze me, Caroline. What's it called?'

'*I'm Throwing My Arms Around Paris*. Quite apt, wouldn't you say?'

He smiled. 'I guess I should wrap my arms around you, then.'

Daniel twirled me around, then pulled me in and held me tight as we swayed to the music.

'I love you,' he whispered into my neck as he softly kissed it.

'I love you too, Daniel.'

'Not now...' he growled over my shoulder.

'Huh? Who you talking too?'

I peered over my shoulder, saw nothing, so looked back at Daniel; a look of horror was etched on his face.

'Daniel, what is it? Tell me what's wrong?' I demanded. I looked back again, and this time saw Michael striding towards us. 'Daniel, why is Michael here?'

He refused to answer, his gaze focused solely on the angel striding towards us.

Deep down, I knew the answer, though. In fact, I think I had known all along. He had been off all day, and I'd refused to see why. He finally spoke.

'I'm sorry, Caroline. I tried to tell you many times.'

'Obviously not hard enough... How could you keep this from me?' I said and bit my lip.

Michael reached for his arm.

'No!' I pushed Daniel away from his grip.

'Don't make this any harder than it has to be, there's a good girl,' said Michael.

'Don't you dare patronise me,' I spat. 'You aren't as kind as I thought, leaving spirits here to rot.'

Michael rolled his eyes.

'I'll come back and see you as soon as I can, Caroline, I promise,' said Daniel.

'It won't be the same with a few snatched moments here and there. Daniel, we made plans!'

Michael's eyebrows raised at our exchange, but he remained silent at my remark.

'I know, babe. You can do the rest without me. I'll join you when I can.'

A light purple mist appeared and wrapped around him. The

CHAPTER SEVENTEEN

mist swirled and turned to rain. With each droplet that landed upon his skin, a part of him disappeared until he'd vanished completely.

Michael left with a parting wave.

My person, my lover, my friend had lived out his time on this plane. I crumbled and sank to my knees.

Tears fell for Daniel, my future, and the unknown. I hadn't been able to cry since my first day as a spirit, and now I refused to stop.

I don't know how long I stayed in that position until Eisen found me.

'Get up, Caroline,' he coaxed.

'No.' I sniffed, the tears finally subsiding.

'Get up now.'

'Why are you here? Piss off with your secrets and riddles. Haven't you done enough?' I got up and faced him. 'You said find someone to spend my time with, someone I'd already met, and I did that. And now he's gone.'

'Daniel wasn't the person I was referring to.'

'What? Of course, he was. We loved each other.'

Eisen shook his head.

'Then, who?' I asked, perplexed.

'Me.'

'Ew, don't make me laugh,' I scoffed. 'I could never love you, and I'll never believe anything you say again.'

'Not for romance, Caroline. I never once mentioned romance when I spoke to you. You've been tested, and you've passed. Can't you see? Everything that you've done and witnessed has brought you to this moment.'

'Tested? Passed what?'

'You are coming to help me,' he said, folding his arms into a prayer position.

'Help you with what?' I snapped.

'We are going to help Max and the rest of the souls stuck down here.'

The end.

Afterword

If you or someone you know has been affected by issues covered in our book the following organisations may be able to provide help:

Samaritans: 116 123

Cruse Bereavement Care: 0808 808 1677

Printed in Poland
by Amazon Fulfillment
Poland Sp. z o.o., Wrocław